Sudden as the weight of what had happened earlier that day crash down on her. She pressed herself back into her seat, images of Mark and the pixie girl now flooding back to her. Tears began to form, and she struggled to get a handle on her emotions.

"Is something wrong?" Scott asked.

Kenya glanced back at him. Just looking into his deep brown eyes made her relax.

But wait! a voice in her head warned. *How can you possibly be falling for this guy after what Mark did to you? Do you really want to be hurt like that again?*

"I'm fine," Kenya said quickly, willing the tears to hold off for a few more minutes. She had to get away from Scott—*now*. "But I have to go," she told him, heading for the door.

"Wait! Kenya . . ."

Without responding, she stepped outside. Her eyes now welled up, as if the sudden impact had set the tears free.

"Kenya!" she heard Scott shout as the train started to chug away. Kenya wanted to turn around and smile at him. She wanted to tell him that she would love to see him again. But she didn't dare. How could she open her heart to someone when it had just been shattered?

I hate you, Mark, she thought, wiping her damp cheeks with the cuff of her sweater. *I hate you for doing this to me.*

Don't miss any of the books in —the romantic series from Bantam Books!

Trust Me

Kieran Scott

BANTAM BOOKS
NEW YORK·TORONTO·LONDON·SYDNEY·AUCKLAND

RL 6, age 12 and up

TRUST ME

A Bantam Book / April 1998

Produced by Daniel Weiss Associates, Inc.
33 West 17th Street
New York, NY 10011.
Cover photography by Michael Segal.

ISBN: 0-553-48593-8

Published simultaneously in the United States and Canada

Bantam Books are published by Bantam Books, a division of Bantam
Doubleday Dell Publishing Group, Inc. Its trademark, consisting of the
words "Bantam Books" and the portrayal of a rooster, is Registered in
U.S. Patent and Trademark Office and in other countries. Marca
Registrada. Bantam Books, 1540 Broadway, New York, New York 10036.

PRINTED IN THE UNITED STATES OF AMERICA

OPM   0 9 8 7 6 5 4 3 2 1

*To Mom and Jeff for keeping me sane,
and to Erin, the coolest sister on earth,
for acting as volleyball consultant.*

One

One

"KENYA! YOU'RE GRINNING like a moron," Kenya Clarke's best friend, Aimee Wu, scolded as they hopped onto the el train.

"I know," Kenya responded. "Isn't it great?"

"Well, you'd better quit it," Aimee said. "People are starting to stare."

Kenya glanced around the half empty train car and shrugged. There was a guy in the corner who *was* staring at her. He looked as though he hadn't showered in a decade, and he seemed to be mumbling to himself. Kenya got the distinct feeling he wasn't staring just because she was smiling so much. She put a hand on Aimee's arm and steered her to the opposite end of the car, as far away from the creepy guy as possible.

"Can I help it if I'm excited?" Kenya asked as she and Aimee flopped onto the blue plastic seats. "Mark is going to be *so* surprised." Kenya had

1

skipped out on volleyball practice that afternoon in order to come into downtown Chicago and surprise her boyfriend, Mark. The plan was to catch him on his way out of school after debate practice. It was the one-year anniversary of the day they had first kissed, and Kenya wasn't about to let it go by uncelebrated.

"I don't know, Ken," Aimee said as she studied her reflection in a tiny lavender-colored compact. "What if he didn't go to debate? What if he's off somewhere—like, helping little old ladies cross the street or something?"

Kenya rolled her eyes. Aimee always mocked the way Kenya went on about Mark's good deeds and accomplishments. But could Kenya help it if Mark was the perfect all-American guy? He was captain of his debate team and a member of the Young Entrepreneurs of America, and he volunteered at a soup kitchen every Sunday morning. Aimee claimed he did all those things only to pad his college applications, but Kenya knew better. Mark had an awesome heart and was concerned about his future. What was wrong with that?

"It doesn't matter what you say today, Aim," Kenya told her good-naturedly, grabbing the compact from Aimee's hand. "Mark was so disappointed that we weren't going to get to see each other, he'll probably pass out when he sees my fly self walking toward him."

"But of course," Aimee responded with a hint of sarcasm. "Listen, Ken. You know I want you to be happy. I just want to make sure you don't let Mark disappoint you again."

Kenya suddenly felt queasy. "Do you always have to bring that up? I told you, Mark said it was a misunderstanding, and I believe him. I trust him. Why can't you just drop it?"

"Kenya, you caught him in a dark hallway about to kiss some Tyra Banks look-alike when he was supposed to be inside the gym, dancing with you," Aimee said, her voice rising slightly. "How was that a misunderstanding?"

"They were just friends," Kenya insisted. "He introduced me to her, and she didn't seem guilty at all. That would take some serious acting ability."

"Maybe she was an actress," Aimee muttered.

"Okay, this conversation ends here," Kenya said. She trusted Mark and that was that. What would their relationship be if they didn't have trust?

"You're right. I'm sorry. This is supposed to be a good day," Aimee relented.

"Thank you," Kenya responded with a quick nod. She took a deep breath and studied her reflection in the little powder-covered mirror she'd snatched from Aimee. She smoothed her short black curls with the palm of her hand and wiped a smudge of lipstick off the corner of her mouth, wondering for the billionth time that day if she should have gone with a different eye shadow. The lady behind the makeup counter at the mall had insisted that Gold Coast really brought out the bronze under-tones in Kenya's light brown skin—whatever that

3

meant. But Kenya figured the lady was a professional. Plus, she had looked as though she'd stepped straight out of the pages of *Vogue* and into her white lab coat uniform. She must have known what she was talking about. Satisfied, Kenya snapped the compact shut and handed it back to her friend.

Aimee was wearing a baby blue minidress with brown stacked heels. She had a light blue silk scarf with a delicate brown floral pattern tied loosely around her neck. Diamond studs sparkled in her ears, and her long black hair was pulled back in a low ponytail. She looked as sleek and stylish as ever. Kenya glanced down at her own ensemble and sighed. Her black pleated skirt and red fitted sweater with black tights and loafers seemed boring in comparison.

"Hey!" Aimee gasped, sounding horrified. "What's with the long face? What happened to Miss Sunshine? Miss I'm-more-perky-than-a-QVC-hostess?"

Kenya forced a smile. "Wanna get off at the next stop and switch clothes?"

"Ken." Aimee took Kenya's wrists in her hands and stared right into her eyes. "Forget I ever said anything about him. You look absolutely stunning. When Mark sees you his jaw's gonna drop so hard you'll have to pick it up off the sidewalk for him and carry it home."

Kenya laughed at the mental picture Aimee's words created. It was a stretch to imagine Mark having an exaggerated response to anything—he was very reserved. He didn't even like to kiss in public. At first this had bothered Kenya. But then

4

she had realized that if they saved up all their affection for when they were alone . . . Kenya smiled once again, lost in a daydream about her and Mark.

"Oh, God! I don't even want to know what you're thinking about." Aimee grimaced.

Then, without warning, the train lurched to a stop and Kenya was jolted out of her reverie. Through the window she glimpsed a sign that read East Jackson Boulevard, and she jumped out of her seat, still blushing from her thoughts about Mark.

"This is my stop," Kenya said. "Thanks for riding with me."

"No prob," Aimee answered. "I'll take any excuse to go shopping in the city."

Kenya stepped off the train, and the doors slid shut behind her. The air brakes released with a wheezing sound, and Kenya turned to wave as Aimee's window went past. Aimee flashed her a thumbs-up sign and then waved back before she disappeared in a blur.

Now, if only I knew where I was going, Kenya thought, placing her hands on her hips. Drumming her fingers against her side, she tried to concentrate as she headed out of the station. Kenya hardly ever came into the city by herself. Her parents had made her wait until she turned seventeen—which had happened only a few weeks earlier. *I should've thought this through a little better,* Kenya told herself as she skipped down the concrete steps.

Out on the sidewalk, Kenya slipped her mirrored sunglasses onto the bridge of her nose and checked the street signs. Jackson and South Dearborn. That sounded mildly familiar. She knew this was the stop she and Mark had gotten off at the night he had brought her to a basketball game at his school. Now she just had to remember which way to go. Checking her watch, Kenya realized she had plenty of time before debate practice was over. She took off in a random direction, deciding she'd backtrack if she got too lost.

A light breeze tickled the hair on the nape of her neck, and Kenya tilted her head back to take a deep breath. It was a beautiful, sunny early spring day. Most people had their heavy winter coats slung over their arms. A bunch of kids chased one another down the street, shrieking with laughter. A couple breezed by on in-line skates, holding hands as they maneuvered through the crowds. "Ah, the first bladers of spring," Kenya sighed. She giggled at herself—her heart was as light as air.

Kenya swung her arms lazily as she sauntered down the street. She was feeling a bit smug about her surprise plan. Mark would definitely be psyched to see her.

A smile played about her lips as she remembered their phone conversation the night before. He had been so heartbroken that they wouldn't be able to get together until the weekend. His voice had even cracked in a rare show of emotion when he told her he couldn't miss debate.

Suddenly Kenya stopped short. She hadn't been paying attention to where she was going. The street sign across the avenue read East Harrison. The name wasn't even remotely familiar to Kenya.

Girl, she scolded herself, *you'd better get your head on straight or this anniversary is never gonna happen.* She caught her reflection in a shop window and checked out the store's painted sign: Anita's Flowers and Fortunes.

Flowers and fortunes? That seemed like an odd combo. Well, if Anita was a psychic, maybe she could give Kenya directions to Mark's school.

Kenya swung open the glass door and was welcomed by a tiny tinkling of bells and the fragrance of fresh flowers. She felt as if she had wandered into the middle of an elegant jungle. Beautiful arrangements surrounded her, and a soft petal brushed her cheek as she stepped deeper into the shop. New Age music played softly from hidden speakers, and there was a faint smell of incense that was almost masked by the flowers. Everything was perfectly still.

Kenya started when she heard a voice.

"A colorful arrangement for a lovely lady?"

She looked down to find an impossibly petite old woman smiling up at her from behind a counter. As a volleyball player, Kenya was used to being taller than people, but this lady was definitely the shortest adult she had ever seen.

And those eyes.

They were ice blue, and even though the woman was smiling, her eyes seemed to sear right through Kenya's soul.

"Um . . . I—I, uh . . . ," Kenya stammered. She

7

grabbed a bouquet of tiger lilies and slapped them on the counter. Why did this wrinkled little old lady make her so nervous?

"Big date?" the woman asked in a soft voice as she tied a purple ribbon around the flowers.

"You could say that," Kenya answered tentatively. "Do you think these would be good for a guy?" Kenya gestured at the lilies. Maybe if she made conversation, she would relax a little.

"Oh, yes." The woman grinned at her. "Very manly."

Kenya held out a few bills. As their hands touched, the old woman's expression suddenly turned to a frown. Her fingertips were ice cold. A chill shot through Kenya's arm, and she jerked her hand back.

"He's not good enough for you, dear," the wrinkled old woman muttered. Her piercing eyes fixed on Kenya's face.

Kenya tried to speak, but she couldn't find her voice. Did this woman make a habit of scaring all her customers to death?

Kenya grabbed the flowers and hurried out of the store, fleeing into the fresh air and sunshine. Her head felt foggy. *What a freak!* she thought. *Does she really think she can know anything about Mark just from brushing my fingers? Someone should sic the psycho patrol on her.* Kenya shook her head, banishing the odd encounter from her thoughts. This was supposed to be a good day.

It wasn't until she reached the corner that she

realized she had forgotten to ask for directions. She smacked her palm against her forehead. *How could a guy like Mark possibly be in love with an airhead like me?* she wondered.

Kenya found a completely unscary-looking hot-dog vendor and got directions. She was pleasantly surprised to find out she was only two blocks away from the school. The time on a church clock caught her eye, and she realized she was running late. As she rushed along she tried to decide how she should approach Mark. *Maybe I'll just yell out "Happy anniversary" and let him run over to me and sweep me up in his arms,* she thought, playing the scene out in her mind. *Or maybe I'll sneak up behind him, stick the flowers in his face, and whisper in his ear.* Kenya giggled nervously as she turned a corner.

She spotted the familiar redbrick building down the street and stopped to straighten her skirt. Her heart was pounding in anticipation, and she took a few deep breaths to calm herself down. Suddenly a big crowd of kids came pouring out the front door, chattering and laughing as they split up into smaller groups. Kenya spotted Mark's tall frame and felt a smile light her face. She started walking slowly toward him, deciding on the sneaky approach. A few more students splintered away from the crowd, providing Kenya with an unobstructed view of her boyfriend. She stopped dead in her tracks.

Mark was leaning over to talk to a very pretty, very petite redhead with delicate curls framing her face. He was leaning in close—too close. Kenya's heart lurched as she watched the girl's hair brush Mark's cheek as he pulled away. The girl giggled flirtatiously, as if he had just whispered something sweet in her ear.

No way is this happening to me, Kenya told herself. *I'm overreacting. It looks worse than it is.* Sweat had formed on her palms, causing her hand to stick to the crinkly plastic wrapped around the flowers.

Then, as if to mock her confidence, Mark leaned over and planted a lingering, passionate kiss on the pixie girl's lips.

Hot tears sprang to Kenya's eyes. She stifled a sob in the back of her throat before it turned into an audible wail. *He never kisses in public,* she thought irrationally. *He never even holds hands at the movies.* Her mind whirled, trying to get a grasp on what was happening, frantically searching for an explanation.

In a flash she remembered her conversation with Aimee on the el. *I told you, Mark said it was a misunderstanding, and I believe him. I trust him.* How could she have been so stupid as to believe Mark's lies?

A car horn honked, and Kenya saw Mark and the pixie girl look up and wave at the driver of a silver Mercedes. Kenya stood there, detached, as if she were watching a play onstage. Mark walked the pixie girl to the car, opened the door for her, and gently closed it once she was inside. He couldn't have been more than ten yards away. Yet he was totally unaware that Kenya was right there, both mortified and fighting to control the fiery rage inside her.

As the car pulled away, Mark turned and looked up—right into Kenya's tear-filled eyes. For a split second his lips twitched in a half smile. But then his mouth dropped open. He looked completely stricken—as if someone had just slapped him in the face.

I feel the same way, Kenya thought, frozen in place by shock. Then, suddenly, she felt energized by his horrified expression.

There he was: Mark Wilson, God's gift to guidance counselors, a college admission board's dream come true, standing there in his perfect little private-school blazer, with a perfect crease down the front of his slacks and his perfect black buzz-cut hair and his perfect teeth, with a smudge of that pixie girl's lipstick staining the side of his mouth. Kenya saw through it all for the first time.

Mark Wilson was nothing. Absolutely nothing. Except maybe a liar and a cheat.

Kenya took a deep breath and started walking toward the guy who had been her boyfriend for an entire year. She marveled at how calm she felt. *I'm numb,* she realized as she looked him directly in the eye.

He was inches away.

"Kenya . . . I—I can explain . . . ," Mark stammered lamely.

Sure you can, Mr. Debate Team Captain. Kenya lifted the bouquet of tiger lilies the eerie old lady had sold her just minutes before. A very intuitive old lady, as it turned out.

Mark flinched at the sudden movement, and Kenya smiled wryly. *He thought I was going to hit him*, she thought. *Maybe I should.* Instead, she whipped the flowers to the ground, and they hit his feet with a snap. Petals flew in all directions.

"Happy anniversary," she said through clenched teeth, fixing him with the fiercest glare she could muster.

Mark stared at his feet for a moment, as if the broken flowers surrounding his shoes were the most fascinating things on the planet. Then he slowly raised his eyes and looked at Kenya. "I don't know what to say except I'm sorry," Mark said evenly. His sudden composure only fueled Kenya's anger. *Why does he always have to be so in control?* she thought.

"Save it for someone who cares," Kenya said tersely. She turned on her heel and walked away with her chin held high. Summoning up all the strength she could find, she managed to make it safely around the corner.

Only then did she allow the tears to flow.

TWO

KENYA WANDERED ALONG the sidewalk, staring at the ground. Absently she realized she had never really looked at the ground before. In the past few minutes she'd found at least a dollar in change, a gold chain, and an unwrapped candy bar. She hadn't bothered to pick any of it up. Her limbs felt as if they weighed a hundred pounds each. Walking was taking a lot of effort. Bending down probably would have caused her to pass out from exhaustion.

How could this happen to me? Kenya thought. She wiped her damp cheek with the back of her hand.

She and Mark had spent practically every weekend together for the past year. Had he been seeing someone else the entire time? Had he actually been dating that supermodel-type girl from the dance?

Kenya sniffled and looked up at the sun. It was

entirely possible, she realized. He lived in the city. He went to a different school, had different friends and different interests. He could have been doing anything with anyone while she was tucked safely away in the suburbs, pining away for her perfect boyfriend.

She remembered all the times she had invited him to come see her play in a match and he had told her he had to be at some meeting or another. Then there was that time she had wanted to come into the city to see him debate in the championships. He had told her he would be too nervous if she was there. Had it been just an excuse? Maybe he'd simply wanted to avoid having her in the same room with the pixie girl and the supermodel. *I can't believe how blind I've been!*

Kenya stopped in front of a boutique window displaying a colorful assortment of spring clothes. Standing up close to the glass, she could see her reflection very clearly. She was a mess. She wished there were some way to get hold of Aimee. She'd make Kenya straighten up and stop feeling sorry for herself. Aimee would tell her she was too good for Mark anyway and that she didn't need him in the first place. Kenya Clarke didn't need a guy like that to make her happy.

I don't need a guy at all, Kenya thought. "That's it. I'm not going to waste one more minute thinking about that loser," she said out loud.

Her sudden outburst startled a couple of younger girls who had been looking in the same window, and they inched away. Embarrassed, Kenya smiled at them and lifted her chin. She adjusted the strap of her backpack and squared her shoulders. Checking her watch, she realized she'd been wandering around for almost an hour. It was time to go home and put this horrible day behind her.

Kenya took a few steps and suddenly felt her stomach turn.

She could have sworn she had just seen a petite girl with red curls bound out of a Mercedes and into a store less than half a block away. *It's not possible,* she thought. *I'm just seeing things because I'm still in shock or something. That's totally normal, right?*

"Well, there's one way to find out," she said, straightening up and running her hand over her hair. A guy talking on a cell phone shot her an irritated look. *I have to stop talking to myself,* Kenya thought. Determined to find the redhead, Kenya walked over to the store: Shaw's Bookshop.

The door swung open, and a few people exited. Kenya held the door for them and walked into the shop, having absolutely no clue what she would do if she actually came face-to-face with the girl.

The musty smell of old books mixed with the scent of fresh coffee. The place was huge—she stood on a carpeted walkway in a high-ceilinged room lined with bookshelves that seemed to go on forever. There were bins of used paperbacks stretching down the center of the walkway, and on either side were mazes of polished wooden shelves. A large directory with handwritten categories and arrows pointing in all directions loomed in front of her. Kenya had no idea which way the pixie girl might have gone, so she just took off in the most logical direction: straight ahead.

As she walked, Kenya thought how this would be a cool place to visit under other circumstances. A group of students in college sweatshirts were gathered around a table—Kenya couldn't hear what they were saying, but she could tell they were arguing very passionately about something. An elderly gentleman was sitting in an overstuffed velvet chair, reading quietly to his granddaughter. She couldn't help smiling at them as she walked by, and the man looked up and winked in her direction. Kenya started to cheer up. She almost forgot what had brought her here in the first place.

Suddenly she heard a giggle from her left. She turned around and entered one of the mazes of shelves, trying to discern which direction the sound had come from. She just knew it was the pixie girl. And when she found her she was going to . . . well, she was going to do something.

Kenya tiptoed along, peeking through the space in between the tops of books and the bottoms of shelves. She scanned every aisle and found a lot of people, but she didn't see any red-haired girls. In all the excitement of the hunt, Kenya wasn't looking where she was going and tripped over a shopper who was crouching down to check out a lower shelf. Kenya didn't hit the ground, but she knocked the poor unsuspecting girl over. Kenya muttered an apology and turned to leave. *Let it go,* she told herself. *This whole thing is pointless anyway.*

Kenya brushed off her tights and looked around to find her way back to the front door. With a start she realized she was in the middle of the romance section. Brightly colored books packed the shelves, taunting her with their romantic titles: *The Truest Love, Forbidden Passion, The Other Woman.*

She had to get out of there pronto.

Kenya turned blindly, poised to run—and smacked right into another shopper. This time she fell on her butt and sent the other guy sprawling.

And the hits just keep on coming, Kenya thought.

Scott Hutson covered his face with his arms, his books clattering to the floor around him.

He felt as if he had just been hit by a freight train. One minute he'd been rushing back to the cash register, and the next he was lying flat on his back with a sharp object sticking into his spine. *Ow! What is that, anyway?*

He sat up, twisted slightly at the waist, and found a tiny nail file resting innocently on the carpet. Next to his hip was a lipstick and a small red wallet. Scott followed the trail of female debris with his eyes and found an overturned black bag near his feet. A girl in a black miniskirt and red sweater was crouching nearby, gathering his books in a pile. Scott studied her athletic form.

She must have been the freight train.

"Wow!" Scott said, glancing around. "When you decide to go somewhere, you don't mess around."

"I am so sorry," the freight train said without looking up. She had stacked his books neatly next to a stepladder and was busy gathering her own things. Scott noticed her hands were shaking.

"Hey, it's okay," he said, standing up. "No broken bones or anything." He reached down and offered her his hand. She looked at it for a second and then stood up without his help. She was tall— almost as tall as he was—and now he looked her directly in the eyes.

His heart flipped.

They were the most beautiful, bright brown eyes he had ever seen. He held her gaze for a moment—a long moment.

The girl reached out and handed him his stack of books. She glanced down at the title on top. "*Discovering the Image*?" She looked at him quizzically. He reached out and took the books without looking. He couldn't tear his eyes from her face.

"Um . . . uh . . . yeah," he managed to say. *Really swift,* he thought. *Get it together, Scotty.* "I mean, yes," he said with more confidence. "I'm a photographer. Well, more of a photography student. These books are for my term project at school."

"Really?" she asked. Scott was pleased to see she seemed interested. "Do you go to the University of Chicago?"

Scott laughed. "No. I'm still in high school."

"Sorry again," she said, raising her shoulders. "I

don't seem to be getting anything right today."

A sad, wistful look crossed her face, and Scott impulsively wanted to reach out and put his arm around her. He fought the urge. *She'd probably deck me again,* he thought.

"So, where were you going in such a hurry?" he asked as they made their way back toward the registers.

"Oh!" She seemed startled by the question. "Nowhere, actually. I'm just a little spacy, I guess. You ever get like that?"

"You don't even wanna know," Scott answered. They had reached the front of the store, and he placed his purchases on the green marble countertop. "I do happen to know the perfect cure for spaciness, though."

"Really?" She grinned, and his heart flipped again. Her smile was almost as pretty as her eyes. "And what might that be?" she asked.

"Chocolate milk shakes from Miller's." He handed the clerk a few bills and accepted his change. "It's this place right down the street that sells, like, nothing but burgers and shakes. And these are the best shakes in the world—thick, smooth, and, best of all, cheap. If you're interested, I'll treat."

Scott took his bag and walked over to hold the door open for the freight train.

"How do chocolate milk shakes cure spaciness?" she asked, stepping out onto the street and placing a pair of funky sunglasses over her eyes.

"It's the caffeine in the chocolate mixed with the sugar," he answered matter-of-factly. "It's better than coffee and doesn't have that disgusting aftertaste."

"In that case, maybe we'd better get some before I try to find my way home." She smiled. "I might end up at Wrigley Field instead."

"Great." Scott started off in the direction of Miller's.

"Um, by the way," she said from behind him, "my name's Kenya Clarke."

Scott cringed. *Nice move,* he thought. *Practically throw yourself at the girl's feet and beg her to let you buy her a milk shake and then don't even introduce yourself.* He turned around and walked back to where she was standing.

"Talk about spacy," he said. "I'm Scott Hutson."

He thrust his hand out and she took it, giving it a firm shake.

"It's very nice to meet you," she said, grinning. "Now let's go to work on this milk-shake theory."

Scott yanked a paper napkin from the dispenser and covered his face with it as he struggled to keep from laughing. *Any second now I'm going to spit chocolate all over her and this pseudodate will be history,* he thought.

He and Kenya were both working on their second milk shake and neither of them had stopped laughing since the moment they'd sat down in the back corner booth of the cozy diner. A middle-aged couple sitting at the counter had been yelling at each other in Italian for the past fifteen minutes. Kenya kept commenting sarcastically on how impressed she was that Scott had taken her to such a romantic spot even though they had just met. Scott had responded that he'd known the duct-tape-covered orange vinyl seats would really impress her.

"Do you know what I love most about this place?" Kenya sighed dramatically as the Italian couple turned the volume up another notch.

"What's that, dear?" Scott played along.

"The peaceful atmosphere," Kenya answered, batting her eyelashes at him comically. A ceramic plate—coming from the direction of the Italian couple—shattered against the wall, and Kenya and Scott both jumped.

"Whaddaya say we blow this pop stand?" Scott asked, leaning forward so he could be heard over the din.

"I thought you'd never ask," she responded.

Scott threw a couple of bills on the table and grabbed her hand. She seemed to hesitate for a moment, but as they inched closer to the irate couple her fingers tightened around his. Scott stepped in front of Kenya as the woman picked up another dish and pulled her arm back.

"Run for it!" Scott shouted, and Kenya bolted for the door. He followed close behind and jumped out onto the sidewalk. The plate shattered against the wall right where his head had been a moment earlier.

"Well, I'll give you one thing," Kenya said. "That definitely woke me up."

Scott laughed and hoisted his backpack onto his

shoulder. "I know a place we could go that's actually peaceful," he said.

"I don't know," Kenya said slowly. "I really should be getting home."

"Oh." Scott was disappointed. "Where do you live? Not that you have to tell me or anything. I'm just curious."

"That's okay," Kenya answered, smiling that incredible smile. "I live in Oak Hills. It's a suburb just outside of—"

"No way!" Scott exclaimed. "I'm from Harrisburg!"

"You're kidding. That's unreal! We're in the same division."

"Division?" he asked.

"Yeah. Sports. You know, balls, nets, fields, that kind of thing?"

Scott's face flushed. "I *know* sports," he said. "I just wasn't thinking about . . . forget it. The point is, we take the same train home. There's an eight-thirty—that would give us plenty of time."

"Time to do what?" she asked tentatively.

Scott smiled. He knew he had her. "You'll see."

Three

"YOU WANT ME to go in there?" Kenya shot a wary look at Scott. She was standing in front of a modern, mirrored building with huge glass doors. Square black letters on the clear panes read Kioko Gallery. Scott stopped in his tracks with one foot on the sidewalk and one on the second step leading to the gallery. Kenya stayed rooted to the asphalt and stared up at him as he turned around.

"Come on. You'll love it." Scott reached down to grab her hand, but Kenya backed away. She felt strangely nervous. She had never actually been in an art gallery before. What if everyone in there could tell that she—an awkward volleyball player from the 'burbs—was totally out of her element? She watched as two sleek-looking women decked out in head-to-toe black and chunky silver bracelets disappeared through the doors. Scott followed her gaze.

"Afraid of the fashion police?" he asked, raising an eyebrow and cocking his head.

"I'm not afraid." Kenya hesitated. "I just don't think art is my thing."

"This kind of art is," he insisted. He caught her wrist between his fingers before she had a chance to yank it away again. "Don't worry," he added with a laugh. "You look great, and besides, I'm wearing flannel. I'm sure the apparel patrol will take me out first."

Kenya laughed too, and she felt the tension flow out of her shoulders. Since when was she afraid of new experiences anyway? She followed Scott as he bounded up the steps two at a time and pushed open the doors. He obviously hung out here all the time. And if he was comfortable among art people, she might as well pretend to be a sophisticated gallery hopper too. Besides, Scott had done a great job of keeping her mind off Mark for the past hour or so. Why back out on him now?

It was cool and quiet inside the gallery, just like the museums Kenya had been dragged to on field trips when she was little. But somehow this place was different. Something was missing. As she followed Scott deeper into the wide, open gallery room, Kenya realized what it was.

All around her, the walls were covered with framed photographs. They were different styles and sizes: color, black and white, shaded, panoramic, extreme close-up. But that was all there was—just photography. No sculptures made out of used computer parts and melted Tupperware. No glorified finger paintings in gilded frames screaming out for bizarre interpretations. Just an array of real-life images.

"Kenya," Scott called softly from an open doorway. "In here." Then he disappeared. She entered the other room, this one even larger than the first. The pictures were displayed on cloth-covered dividers that looked like large easels. They were set up in rows across the room, forming a kind of hallway. Kenya could see people's feet and hear whispering voices floating from behind the dividers. But she didn't see Scott.

Suddenly she felt a tap on her shoulder, and she jumped.

"Don't *do* that!" she cried, whacking Scott on the shoulder.

A middle-aged woman with glasses perched on the tip of her nose peered around one of the dividers. "Would you mind keeping your voice down?" she hissed in a pinched, nasal voice.

"Sorry," Kenya whispered, shrugging.

Scott grinned. "Afraid I was the women in black coming to take you away?"

Kenya laughed and shook her head.

Scott started walking along the wall, and Kenya followed. "I guess this place isn't very conducive to conversation," he whispered to her over his shoulder.

"Well, you said it was peaceful," Kenya answered. "I kind of like it."

She noticed they were walking at the same pace, her loafers keeping time with his sneakers as they made their way across the shiny marble floor. *Click, squish. Click, squish.*

"This is my favorite exhibit," Scott said, stopping in front of a set of photographs.

"Oh, wow! This is so cool," Kenya murmured. She studied the colorful collection. Each frame held a crisp photo of a different kind of door. One photo showed a huge wooden barn door with a gaping, jagged hole cut out right near the rusted metal handle. Another picture portrayed a large set of red doors with cracking paint, framed by a jungle of forest green ivy. Each photograph had a card underneath it with the name of the country in which it had been taken.

"This one is the coolest," Scott said, crouching down and pointing to one of the photos. Kenya squatted next to him, touching her fingertips to the floor for balance. It was a Dutch door, its top half open, painted a flawless white and set against a white wooden house. At first there didn't really seem to be anything particularly interesting about it. But when Kenya looked closer, she saw the tops of two little blond heads peeking up over the bottom half of the door. The children must have been standing on their tiptoes in an attempt to see over the edge. Kenya could just make out their little pink fingertips, gripping the door for support.

"How cute," Kenya whispered. "I didn't peg you for the sentimental type." She elbowed him in the ribs as they stood.

"I think all photographers are sort of sentimental,"

Scott said, looking thoughtful. "I mean, all we do is capture moments, make memories—you know?"

"I never thought of it that way," Kenya said, noting how cute Scott looked when he was concentrating. A little crinkle formed right between his eyebrows. Flustered by her thoughts, Kenya looked back at the doors.

"This is my favorite," she said, touching the frame of a photograph. The door was bright turquoise and had a crescent moon cut out of the middle. It was rounded at the top and framed by stark white stones against a blinding yellow wall. Tropical flowers in bright pink hues grew wildly around the base. She checked the card underneath. "Caribbean door," she read aloud with a sigh.

"Of course." Scott nodded. "It's just like you—full of color."

Kenya felt an intense blush rising on her cheeks and glanced at Scott out of the corner of her eye. He looked back at her, then blushed himself.

"Let's check out the landscape display. I hear they have some great new mountain ranges." Scott turned away abruptly, obviously nervous.

Kenya took a deep breath and tried to squelch the butterfly war that was going on in her stomach. *Am I insane?* she thought. She hadn't even officially broken up with Mark yet—although that relationship clearly was as over as the grunge look. But still, just a couple of hours before, she had learned for the first time what it felt like to have her heart broken, and it hadn't been especially fun. The pain she'd felt seeing Mark with someone else was still sharp, yet here she was, flirting with a guy she didn't even know.

But then again, he *was* incredibly good-looking. He had the softest brown eyes and thick lashes that any woman would kill for. Even though he was wearing baggy jeans and a flannel shirt over a T-shirt, she could tell he had an athletic form. And that smile! It could melt steel.

Why am I standing here? Kenya thought suddenly, moving to look for him. *I'm letting him get away!*

This time she found Scott sitting on a black backless bench, gazing at a huge framed photo. She dropped down next to him, tucking her feet under the bench. The picture that had caught his attention was of a beautiful snow-covered mountain range set against an incredibly vivid, cloudless blue sky. The colors were unbelievably stark—the scene hardly looked real.

"I'd kill to go there," Scott sighed without taking his eyes off the photograph.

"I dunno," Kenya answered, shrugging out of her backpack and swinging it to the floor in front of her. "That Caribbean door is more my speed. I'm not a big fan of snow."

Scott looked at her with surprise. "You must *love* living in Chicago, then," he joked.

"Mmm," she murmured. She grabbed a small tub of lip balm out of the zipper pouch of her bag and touched up her lips. "Yeah. Winter's not my thing. My lips and skin are *always* dry. But in the winter? Forget it! I'm beyond moistureless. You probably couldn't even grow a cactus on me."

Scott chuckled and shook his head.

"Do you want to have your pictures displayed here someday?" Kenya asked.

"That would be incredible," he said wistfully. "You know, my dad used to have shows here all the time."

"Shows?" Kenya asked.

"It's when they dedicate a night to one artist," Scott explained. "Then they'll usually feature that person's work in one room of the gallery for a month or so. It's a pretty big deal. If you land a show at a well-respected gallery, you have a chance of getting noticed by a collector or an art critic, and then anything can happen."

"Wow. So, your dad's a hotshot photographer?"

"Was," Scott answered, focusing on the floor. Then he picked his head up and looked Kenya directly in the eyes. "He passed away about a year ago,"

"I'm so sorry," Kenya said without flinching, though her heart went out to Scott. She could tell his dad had meant a lot to him, and still did. He was even following in his father's footsteps. They were both silent for a moment.

"Well. This is a rockin' good time, isn't it?" Scott said suddenly, cracking a grin. He stood up and took a deep breath. "Let's get out of here." He picked up Kenya's backpack and handed it to her. "We don't get many nice spring days around here. We'd better enjoy it while we can."

"Yes," Kenya responded, standing up and laughing. "Before the clock strikes winter once again and I turn back into a dried-up alligator."

"One with kraut and mustard," Scott ordered, grabbing a few napkins from a pile on the hot-dog vendor's cart. "You want anything, Kenya?" he asked.

"Are you kidding? What are you, a bottomless pit?" Kenya joked, stepping down from the curb she had been using as a balance beam. She couldn't imagine ever eating again after the two enormous shakes she had consumed that afternoon. She felt as if she were going to burst out of her skirt.

"I'm a growing boy," Scott argued, taking a huge bite out of his hot dog and spilling a heap of sauerkraut on the grass.

"Guys." Kenya threw up her hands in mock exasperation.

Scott started to shove his wallet into his back pocket with one hand while balancing his hot dog with the other. The billfold slipped from his fingers.

Grinning, Kenya crouched to the ground to pick it up. The wallet had fallen open to a photograph. Kenya studied the picture inconspicuously as she stood. It was a picture of Scott beaming as he held a beautiful girl around the waist. The girl had long, shiny brown hair and a perfect smile. The photo had obviously been taken at a formal dance. Kenya's stomach turned.

"What's so interesting?" Scott asked.

"She's pretty," Kenya commented lightly, handing the wallet back. "Is she your girlfriend?"

Scott laughed loudly. "Emma? No way," he said, successfully replacing the wallet this time. "She's just a friend. Neither one of us wanted to deal with finding a real date for the winter formal, so we went together. A lot of our friends did the same—we hung out together most of the night."

Kenya studied Scott's face for a second, trying to discern whether or not he was telling the truth. He took a huge bite of his hot dog, and another blob of sauerkraut fell to the ground with a splat. If he was lying, he sure wasn't displaying any signs of guilt.

Why would he lie? Kenya thought, starting to walk across the park. *So what if that girl is totally beautiful? It's not like Scott is Mark. And it's not like you're going out with him—he has no reason to lie.* Kenya took a deep breath and felt her doubts disappear. *Relax. You've just met him—you're having a good time with him for the afternoon and that's all.*

Dusk was falling as they cut across Grant Park on their way to the train station. Kenya heard the crack of a baseball bat and watched as a little boy ran the bases on a nearby field. His mom snapped a picture as he got to third base. He waved at his mom, grinning like crazy.

"He's cute," Kenya said. "He almost looks like—" She stopped abruptly and bit her lip. The boy looked like a younger version of Mark.

"Like who?" Scott asked.

"Oh, um, no one," Kenya answered, fighting

back the feelings of loss that were growing inside her. For the past year Mark had been so present in her thoughts. . . .

"So, are you definitely going to be a photographer?" Kenya asked, determined to force Mark out of her mind. She looked over at Scott, who was struggling to avoid losing any more sauerkraut.

He nodded. "Actually, I'm applying for a summer internship at the *News-Tribune*," Scott said, referring to their local county paper.

"Really? That sounds pretty cool." Kenya kicked at a stone with the tip of her shoe. "Would you, like, get to cover late-breaking stories and all that?"

"As a high-school intern, I'd probably get to cover things a little bit less exciting. Like this, for example." Scott gestured at the Little League baseball game. "But I wouldn't mind. It would be great practice, and it would be so cool to actually get paid to take pictures. I mean, it's what I do for fun."

Scott balled up his napkin and threw it in the direction of a green trash can, missing the mark by at least two feet. He hung his head.

"Not much of a basketball player, are you?" Kenya teased.

Scott looked at her with an amused smile. "Enough about me," he said, deftly changing the subject. "What do you want to be when you grow up, Ms. Clarke?"

"That," Kenya said, pointing in the direction of a volleyball game that was going on in the middle of the lawn.

"You want to be a mime?" Scott sounded genuinely shocked.

Kenya glanced back at the game, confused, and then cracked up. Behind the volleyball players, a mime dressed in a black bodysuit and a beret was performing for a group of little kids. "Ah, no," Kenya said. "I was referrring to the volleyball players."

"Really?" Scott sounded even more surprised.

Kenya was immediately offended. Why were guys always stunned when a girl wanted to pursue athletics? "For your information, Mr. I'm-too-cool-because-I'm-a-photographer, I was the first person in the history of our division to play varsity volleyball as a freshman. I've been on the all-state team twice and I'm well on my way to a third time. And—"

"Hey!" Scott threw his hands up in surrender. "I didn't mean anything by it. I'm actually impressed."

"Impressed?" Kenya crossed her arms over her chest and struck a defensive pose. She eyed him skeptically, wondering if she could believe him.

"Yeah. I mean, I'm horrible at sports, so I admire anyone who plays something well enough to want to make a career out of it," Scott said. He ran his hand over his short hair and shifted his weight from one foot to the other, looking nervous.

"Maybe you just haven't found the right sport yet." Kenya's tone of voice was now much calmer. She felt bad for blowing up at Scott and didn't want him to be uncomfortable. But there was that cute crease between his brows again. *I should try to make him squirm more often*, she thought.

"Maybe you're right," Scott responded, visibly more relaxed. Kenya started to stroll around the volleyball court, and he followed her lead. "I do a lot of hiking when I'm taking pictures, but that's practically all the exercise I get. Everyone wanted me to play basketball because I'm tall, but—as you've already seen—I'm no Shaquille O'Neal."

"Shaq you are not," Kenya agreed, shaking her head.

"But maybe if I found the right volleyball coach . . ." He grinned at her mischievously.

Kenya stopped and took an appraising look at Scott. She stroked her chin between her thumb and forefinger, as if she were gauging his potential.

"I think you have the perfect body for volleyball," she said finally.

"Perfect body, huh?" Scott grinned.

Kenya felt her cheeks grow warm. He didn't miss a beat, did he? But she had to admit that with his broad shoulders and long legs, he did look pretty flawless. Plus, he was sweet, attentive, intelligent, and funny. She wondered how Mark would react if he knew she had ended up spending the afternoon with such an incredible guy. Scott Hutson was revenge personified. *Eat your heart out, Mark Wilson.*

"Come on, photo boy," she said, hooking her arm through his. "The sun is starting to go down. If we don't get a move on, we're going to miss the train."

"And would that be so bad?" he asked as he fell into step with her.

Kenya laughed, feeling genuinely happy. "No, I

guess it wouldn't be so bad," she agreed, smiling into his handsome face.

Not bad at all.

"We're never gonna make it!" Kenya heard Scott yell as she dodged her way through the crowd at the Randolph Street station. She could hear the soles of his sneakers smacking against the ground behind her.

"Oh, yes we are!" she shouted without looking back. Her backpack slapped against her butt as she ran, and she cursed herself for wearing it with the straps so loose—her backside was going to be bruised for weeks. Kenya hurdled over a suitcase that was sitting in the middle of the terminal. She spotted their track up ahead. Their train was still there.

"Final call for the eight-thirty County Line train, now boarding on track three," the loudspeaker blared.

"We're never gonna make it," Scott repeated.

"Oh, yes we are," Kenya answered again.

Scott was neck and neck with her now, and out of the corner of her eye Kenya could see him sprinting. *Nice form,* she noted.

A huge pack of tourists shuffled along, looking around and checking their maps of Chicago. They seemed totally oblivious to the fact that Kenya and Scott were bearing down on them at top speed. Kenya shot a look at Scott, and he gave a slight nod. They parted, each running around a different side of the crowd. When they rejoined, they almost missed their track—Scott had to reach out and grab Kenya's arm, pulling her into the turn.

The train was pulling away.

"Come on, kids!" a portly conductor with scruffy white hair yelled from the door of the second car. He tipped his hat back and waved them on encouragingly.

"We're never gonna make it," Scott panted, adding a little burst of speed.

"Would you stop saying that?" Kenya spat, keeping pace with him and trying to control her labored breathing.

Scott reached out and grabbed the handrail at the door of the last car. He leaped and planted his feet on the bottom step. Then he turned and thrust out his hand to Kenya. She grabbed his outstretched arm with one hand and grabbed the bar with the other, hoisting herself up. The train lurched, and she latched on to Scott for balance. She paused to catch her breath, clutching the soft fabric of his flannel shirt in her hands.

Scott had moved up one step and Kenya was on the one below him, so her cheek was resting against his T-shirt. She was so close to him, she could feel his heart hammering against his chest and smell the fabric softener on his shirt, mixed with the pungent scent of fresh perspiration. A shiver ran through Kenya's body, and her cheek tingled. She liked being this close to Scott. She liked it a lot.

Scott took a deep breath and exhaled, ruffling the curls on the top of Kenya's head. She looked up at him and then slowly pulled herself away.

"And you said you weren't an athlete," she teased.

"Well, maybe I'm not *totally* helpless," Scott replied. "Let's see if we can find a good seat."

Kenya followed Scott into the car and sat down in the vinyl seat across from him, placing her backpack in the empty space next to her. She slumped down a little and sighed contentedly as the train clattered along. After the insane day she'd had, it was nice to finally be resting.

They were both quiet for a while. Kenya couldn't help stealing glances at Scott. Every once in a while she would catch his eye and they would both look away. Kenya then turned to watch the scenery going by outside her window. She smiled slightly as she thought about how silly they were acting.

"My mom's going to kill me," Scott said suddenly.

"How come?" Kenya asked, crossing her ankles and smoothing her skirt.

"I was supposed to be home about two hours ago," Scott answered, laughing.

"I'm going to be early," Kenya muttered. She remembered how that morning, after much pleading, her mom had begrudgingly given her permission to stay out later than usual on a school night. It was, after all, a special occasion.

"What were you doing in the city anyway?" Scott asked. "You never mentioned."

Suddenly Kenya felt the weight of what had happened earlier that day crash down on her. She pressed herself back into her seat, images of Mark and the pixie girl now flooding back to her. Tears began to form, and she struggled to get a handle on her emotions, which were rapidly spinning out of control. *Quit it!* she scolded herself. *You can't turn into a total basket case in front of this guy.*

"Is something wrong?" Scott asked, leaning forward in his seat.

Kenya glanced back at him, startled by the interruption in her thoughts. There was that awesome brow crease again. Just looking into his deep brown eyes made her relax.

But wait! a voice in her head warned. *How can you possibly be falling for this guy after what Mark just did to you? Do you really want to be hurt like that again?*

"I'm fine," Kenya mumbled.

"You don't look fine," Scott said. "You look like you just lost your best friend." He reached out and touched her knee.

Kenya jumped up into the aisle as if his touch had burned her.

Scott's eyes were wide with confusion. "What did I do?"

"Nothing! I . . . uh, it's just . . ."

"First stop, Anderson Street, Oak Hills," the conductor's voice crackled over the speaker.

"It's just that this is my stop," Kenya blurted out, grateful for the convenient excuse.

"Oh, right." Scott didn't seem entirely convinced. "Well, can I call you sometime?" He dug into his backpack and pulled out a notebook and pen.

Kenya's heart was pounding rapidly. All of a sudden she felt totally trapped and closed in. She had to get away from Scott. She had to get off this train—now. "I don't think that's such a good idea," Kenya said, amazed at how normal her voice sounded.

"Why not?" Scott asked, the surprise in his voice evident.

The train slid into the station and pulled to a stop. Kenya snatched her backpack from the seat and clutched it to her chest.

"I have to go," she said quickly, willing the tears to hold off for a few more minutes. As she headed for the door she glimpsed Scott starting to get out of his seat.

"Wait! Kenya . . ."

Without responding, she dropped to the ground. Her eyes now welled up, as if the sudden impact had set the tears free. She took off across the parking lot awkwardly, her pace slowed by her shaking knees and her blurred vision.

"Kenya!" she heard Scott shout as the train started to chug away. Kenya wanted to turn around and smile at him, the way she had done all afternoon. She wanted to tell him that she would love to see him again. But she didn't dare. How could she open her heart to someone when it had just been shattered?

I hate you, Mark, she thought, wiping her damp cheeks with the cuff of her sweater. *I hate you for doing this to me.*

Four

"SCOTTEEEEEEEEEE!" SCOTT'S LITTLE sister Tracy, arms outstretched, came running toward him the moment he walked through the front door. Scott bent down and scooped her pudgy little body up into a big bear hug.

"How's the munchkin?" he asked, nuzzling his face into her neck and causing her to squeal and squirm. "Huh? How's the munchkin?"

"Munchkin's good!" she said in her little two-year-old voice. "Munchkin helped Mommy with dinner."

"You did?" Scott said, plunking his wiggling sister down on the floor, making sure she was balanced before he let go. She took off, back toward the kitchen.

"Mommeeeeee! Scotty's home!" she squealed. Scott laughed and shook his head. He pulled his backpack off, threw it on the rocking chair near the door, and took a deep breath.

All the way home he'd tried to sort through the weird scene with Kenya on the train. He couldn't for the life of him figure out what he had done wrong. He'd been sure she'd want to see him again after the great time they'd had. He'd even felt awkward asking for her number, because he'd just figured she would offer it to him.

That's what you get for being so full of yourself, he thought, stretching his arms above his head and letting out a groan. He could hear the sounds of pots clattering and water running—his mom was cleaning up after supper. She was going to be really angry with him. He had even missed his dish night. *Well, time to face the music.*

"Man, are you in trouble," Scott's other little sister, Catherine, mocked him as she bounded down the stairs. At ten years old, Cat had outgrown *her* cute phase a long time ago. Now it seemed as though her main function was to make Scott's life miserable. When she wasn't mall-hopping or riding her dirt bike, she was stealing his most expensive camera or swiping his clothes out of the laundry room. Usually he just blew her off, but that night he figured he should pump her for information.

"Is she really mad?" Scott whispered, following his sister over to the couch as she flopped down and snatched up the remote control.

"She made stuffed pork chops, Scott. You figure it out," she responded in a bored tone, not taking her eyes off the television.

"Not with corn bread and beans?" Scott asked.

Catherine nodded tersely and continued to flip channels.

Scott sighed and shut his eyes. He couldn't believe his bad luck. His mom's stuffed pork chops with corn bread and beans was one of his favorite dishes and one of the hardest to prepare. In his house, if you missed dinner on a big-meal night, you were generally done for. He knew he was in for one of those when-I'm-gone-you'll-appreciate-me lectures.

The kicker was, he hadn't even gotten anything out of missing dinner that night. If Kenya hadn't bolted from the train, he wouldn't have minded a lecture so much. But Kenya had left him hanging, and now not only was he confused, he was also in big trouble.

"Scott Hutson!" His mom's voice burst through the open door that connected the living room to the kitchen. "Are you coming in here or are you just going to hide out all night?"

Scott stood up slowly and dragged himself toward the kitchen.

"Heh, heh, heh," Catherine laughed sarcastically as he moved away.

How had this day gone so wrong?

Scott's mother was standing at the sink on the far wall with her back to him. He watched her rinse the last pot and place it on the dish drainer next to lots of dripping cookware. She was wearing jeans and one of his dad's old sweatshirts—her normal after-work attire. Tracy was running around the kitchen table, singing the theme song from *Bananas in Pajamas* and swinging a teddy bear back and forth.

"Hi, Scotty!" she cried as she passed him on one of her laps. Scott smiled at her and then looked up at his mom's back.

"Hi, Mom!" he said brightly. "How was your day?"

Scott's mom dried her hands on a towel, turning to face him. She didn't look happy. "It was fine until I had to wash the dishes," she said.

"Mom, I'm sorry, I—"

"Hold it!" she cut him off. "It's not the dishes I'm upset about, Scott, and you know it. You're getting older now and I don't want to have to lecture you about being responsible. If your plans change for some reason, you call and let me know. You got it?"

"Yeah, I got it," Scott answered. He hung his head and waited for more.

"Good. Now I'm gonna go put my feet up and watch some television with the girls." His mom started to walk past him.

Scott's head popped up. "You mean that's it?" he asked incredulously.

"That's it," she told him, stopping to plant a kiss on his cheek. Then she patted him on the back and left the room, Tracy in tow.

All right! Scott thought, opening the refrigerator in search of leftovers. *My luck is changing. Maybe I should look up Kenya's phone number in the phone book while I'm on a roll.*

"Oh, and Scott?" his mom called from the living room.

"Yeah?"

"Dish duty for two weeks."

He heard Catherine laugh.

Maybe not.

Scott slipped his last photograph into the fixing bath and let out a long sigh. After scarfing down some of his mother's leftovers, he had retired to the darkroom to work on a couple of rolls he'd taken that week. Or at least that was what Scott had told himself. He had actually come up here to think.

Taking a deep breath, Scott sat down in the rolling leather chair and swiveled around in a circle. For the thousandth time he silently thanked his father for having turned what had once been a study into a darkroom. Photos hanging to dry, tubs of solutions, developing mechanisms: this was Scott's haven. It was the only place he could go where no one would disturb him. In the past he'd spent hours up here developing film and thinking about what he was going to do with his future. But now all he could think about was Kenya.

"This is bad," Scott said out loud. "I really can't deal with this right now."

He looked back at all the pictures he had developed, and groaned. Garbage. It was all garbage. He was never going to win the internship position if this was all he had to submit. And then there was the term project he was working on for class, which included turning in a portfolio and a ten-page paper. He was never going to get anywhere if he let himself get distracted by a girl.

The phone rang, and Scott stood up, startled,

not realizing he had left the portable phone in the darkroom. He searched around and found it buried under a pile of old contact sheets.

Scott grabbed the receiver, sending the papers fluttering to the floor. "Hello?"

"Hey! Scotty!"

"What's up?" Scott said, recognizing the voice of his best friend, Jeff Pierce. Scott sank back into his chair.

"How was the city?" Jeff asked.

Scott chewed on the inside of his cheek. Maybe Jeff would have some advice about Kenya. He *had* been on more dates than anyone else Scott knew. "I met a girl, actually," he said.

"Really?" Jeff sounded intrigued. "Are we talking babe or what?"

"Definite babe," Scott said with a laugh. "This is not your average girl." Scott closed his eyes and conjured up an image of Kenya in his mind. He had gotten into the habit of imagining still photographs of people he knew. Many of his memories came in the form of snapshots. "Her name's Kenya and she's incredible. I mean, she wants to be a professional athlete."

I bet she could do it, too, Scott thought. *I've never even seen her play, but I bet she could make the Olympic team and find a way to start some kind of national league at the same time.* Kenya seemed like the kind of girl who could do anything.

"A jock, huh?" Jeff said playfully. "Sounds more like my type than yours."

"No way, she's mine," Scott said, spinning around in his chair.

"All right, all right. I guess I can let you have *one* girl," Jeff teased. "So, are you gonna call her?"

"I don't know, man. I mean, she bolted before I could get her number," Scott said tentatively.

"Oh. That doesn't sound good." Jeff's voice turned serious.

"Yeah, well, the thing is, we were having an awesome time," Scott said. "At least *I* thought we were."

"If you had a good time, she probably did too. I bet she's just messin' with your mind," Jeff said. "I hate it when they do that."

"Me too." Scott stared at the floor. A girl had never bothered to mess with his mind before, but if that was what Kenya was doing, it didn't feel good.

"My advice is, if you really like her, track her down. That's probably what she wants you to do anyway. They love all that romance stuff. Get off the phone right now and call her. If you don't do it now, you'll chicken out for sure."

"Thanks for your support," Scott said sarcastically.

"No problem, man," Jeff responded. Then the line went dead.

Wow, Scott thought. *He wasn't kidding when he said to call her now.*

"Maybe Jeff's right. Maybe I should just call her," Scott muttered, leaning back in his chair. He was about to dial information, but then stopped himself.

Wait, what am I doing? Scott thought, resting his head in his hands.

With everything he had going on in his life, he couldn't afford any complications. *And besides,* he thought, pushing himself out of the chair and beginning to pace, *she doesn't want to have anything to do with me anyway.*

But down deep, he didn't believe that. He had a gut feeling that Kenya had been upset about something that had nothing to do with him. Come to think of it, she had been totally distracted back at the bookstore before she ran into him. *Ran me over is more like it,* Scott thought, smiling wistfully. Images of Kenya popped back into his mind: her timid expression when she had been standing in front of the gallery, her smile when she had made that crack about growing a cactus on her skin, her defiant stance when she'd thought he was mocking her dream to make a career out of volleyball.

Scott crossed the room, removed his photo from the fixer, and hung it with the others, then let out another sigh. He knew he hadn't done anything wrong with Kenya. He'd been the perfect gentleman. "There *must* have been something else bugging her. I have to see her again and make *sure* she really doesn't want to see me," Scott said aloud.

He checked his watch—it was getting late. "Tomorrow," he said. "I will definitely call her tomorrow." He glanced around the messy darkroom again, shaking his head in frustration.

One thing's for sure, he thought, slipping out of the room. *Until I know what's going on with Kenya, my career is going nowhere.*

★　　★　　★

"I can't believe he did this to you!" Aimee fumed, pacing the ivory-colored carpet in Kenya's bedroom.

Rrrrrip! Kenya tore a photo of Mark and herself in half and added it to the small pile that was forming on her bedspread.

"I mean, I *can* believe it, but I can't *believe* it. You know?" Aimee continued. She grabbed up a velvet throw pillow and pounded it with her fist.

Rrrrrip! Kenya scowled as she tore another picture, this one a snapshot of her with a bunch of Mark's friends.

"And then to not even come after you!" Aimee ranted, pitching the pillow back onto the bed.

Kenya stood up and walked over to her bookcase. She pulled down a teddy bear that Mark had given her on Valentine's Day and tossed it onto the photo pile.

"I mean, what a complete slimeball." Aimee stood with her hands on her hips, watching Kenya. "What about your box?" she asked.

"I almost forgot my box!" Kenya exclaimed. She had been vaguely aware of Aimee's rantings and ravings for the past fifteen minutes or so. But she had been so intent on finding every scrap of memorabilia from her relationship with Mark that she hadn't really been paying attention to her. And she couldn't believe she had almost forgotten about her memory box.

Kenya flung open her closet door, pulled the colorful hatbox down from the top shelf, and ceremoniously carried it into the center of her room. She kicked a pair of dirty jeans into the corner and plopped down on the plush carpet. Aimee sat down across from her and folded her legs. Gingerly Kenya lifted the lid from the box and looked down at the familiar collection of ticket stubs, athletic programs, ribbons, and other remnants of her past. She picked up the box with her fingertips and overturned it, dumping its contents in a heap between her friend and herself.

Aimee began picking through the pile.

"Make sure you only get rid of the Mark stuff," Kenya warned her. This box was her life. She often thought that if, heaven forbid, her house was ever on fire, she would risk taking an extra moment to grab her memory box before fleeing.

Kenya picked up a picture of her first volleyball team and ran her fingers reverently across the surface. Looking at her little, innocent, grinning face, she couldn't help smiling. "If only you knew what you were in for," she said to her ten-year-old self.

"Hey!" Aimee exclaimed. "This is no time for reminiscing!" She snatched the photo from Kenya's hands.

"Be careful with that!" Kenya screeched.

"Okay! Okay!" Aimee said, laying the picture carefully to the side. She flicked her ponytail over her shoulder with a manicured nail. "But let's get back to the task at hand."

"Operation Lose the Loser," Kenya deadpanned.

"Exactly." Aimee nodded.

Kenya started to methodically pull items from the colorful mass: A valet parking stub from her birthday dinner. A cassette single of their song. A program from *The Music Man*, in which Mark had played the lead, Harold Hill. *How fitting*, Kenya thought, disgusted.

Good old Harold had been a total fraud too.

Within minutes she and Aimee had made a new pile on the floor to add to the one on her bed.

Aimee stood up and slapped her hands on her thighs. "Mission accomplished," she said, checking her hair in the mirror.

Kenya glanced inside the box, and something sparkly caught her eye. It was the fake ruby ring Mark had won for her during the skeeball marathon they'd had on their first date. A jab of pain shot through Kenya's heart. That had been one of the greatest nights of her life. She sighed heavily. Maybe she didn't have to give up *everything*. She slipped the ring on the her left hand and turned it over so that only the thin fake-gold band was showing. Aimee would never notice it.

"So, what're you going to do with all of it?" Aimee asked, gathering the mess up in her arms and scooting over to the bed on her knees. She added the load to the first heap, forming a rather extensive collection of junk.

"I don't know," Kenya mumbled, feeling overwhelmed. She was experiencing another wave of debilitating exhaustion like the one she had endured that afternoon. "I guess I'll just trash it."

"Not monumental enough," Aimee reasoned. "How about a bonfire in the driveway? Maybe we could find some kind of chant and put a curse on him."

"Yeah, right." Kenya rolled her eyes. "That would sure thrill the parental units." She dropped down on the clean part of her bed, lying on her back.

"I was just kidding, Ken," Aimee said, sitting on the edge of the mattress next to Kenya. "You know, trying to lighten the mood and all."

Kenya sighed again and closed her eyes. She flung her arm over her brow and waited for the images of Mark and the pixie girl to crowd her brain again. Instead, a picture of Scott floated into her mind's eye. She visualized him sitting across from her at Miller's, grinning and cracking jokes. Kenya felt herself start to smile and let out an audible groan. *What am I going to do?*

"It's okay, Kenya," Aimee commiserated, patting her arm. "It doesn't seem like it right now, but you *will* get over him."

"What if I don't want to get over him?" Kenya asked quietly.

"How could you not?" Aimee demanded.

"Not what?" Kenya's eyes flew open.

"Not want to get over Mark!" Aimee seemed exasperated.

"Mark?" Kenya blinked in confusion, sitting up.

"The clueless, good-for-nothing creep who broke your heart this afternoon?" Aimee sounded thoroughly baffled.

"Oh!" Kenya smacked her forehead with her hand. She was definitely breaking some kind of dazed-and-confused record today. Aimee had been talking about Mark while her own mind had been on Scott. "I have something to tell you," Kenya said.

"What is it?" Aimee's voiced turned serious, picking up her friend's tone.

51

"I met this guy today. . . ."

"You *what?*" Aimee jumped up. "When? Where? Before or after the pixie girl?"

Kenya laughed and started to explain. She told Aimee all about Scott—how incredibly handsome he was, how hilariously funny and interesting and athletic, even though for some reason he didn't think so. By the time she was done, Aimee was sitting next to her on the bed again, clutching the velvet pillow and gazing at her in rapt attention.

"Kenya," she breathed. "He sounds amazing. Don't dwell on the past—that's what I always say. You can throw this right back in Mark's face. This is so awesome!"

"Awesome? It's horrible!" Kenya wailed. She fell backward onto the bed again, causing a bunch of photo scraps to flutter to the floor.

Aimee leaned forward and felt Kenya's forehead with the back of her hand. "Are you running a delusion-inducing fever or are you just genetically insane?" Aimee asked.

"I'm not crazy!" Kenya protested, pushing Aimee's hand away and rolling onto her side. "I went out with Mark for an entire year. I thought we were the perfect couple. And now I find out I couldn't trust him as far as I could throw him."

"If you ask me, I think you could throw that jerk pretty darn far."

"Aimee!" Kenya laughed and hit her friend over the head with another pillow.

"Okay!" Aimee said, throwing her hands up in

surrender. "But I think you're nuts to assume you can't trust this guy just because Mark turned out to be a total zero." Aimee stood and straightened the hem of her fitted T-shirt. "Which is something I've been aware of for quite some time, I might add."

"I guess you're right," Kenya said, bending over and gathering her Mark debris into a more compact pile. "But it doesn't matter anyway. I don't even have his phone number."

"That is what phone books are for, my friend," Aimee told her. She pulled the garbage can out from under Kenya's desk and placed it next to the bed. Kenya swept the pile into the can with the side of her arm.

"Yo! Kenya!"

Kenya looked up. Her brother, Darrel, was standing in the doorway of her room, wearing a pair of neatly pressed slacks and a silk shirt. His shoes were buffed to the point of shining, and he was carrying a bouquet of roses.

"Not bad!" Aimee said, then whistled. She crossed her arms in front of her and eyed Darrel up and down.

"Eat your heart out, Wu," Darrel said, executing a little twirl. "Ken, are you feeling any better?"

"Much," Kenya answered with a quick nod.

"Good, 'cause you were really wiggin' me out before with all that 'I hate men' stuff," Darrel said, laughing. "Whatever Mark did must've been pretty bad. I was ready to come in here with a straitjacket, but Mom said I should leave you alone—"

"Mom!" Kenya broke in suddenly. Before she had called Aimee, Kenya had spent a good ten minutes throwing a tantrum in her room. The thought that her family might have heard her had never even crossed her mind. "I'm such a bad daughter. She must be freaking out, wondering what's wrong."

"Pretty much," Darrel agreed. "You should really go down there and talk to her. She's watching *Happy Days* reruns, and you know what that means."

"*Happy Days*?" That was bad. Kenya's mom never watched TV unless it was OMNI or the Discovery Channel. Her dad was a TV fanatic, but he was away on a business trip that week. When he was gone, the Clarke household was usually pretty quiet. Kenya's mom would normally have her head buried in a book or an educational magazine. *Happy Days* meant she was totally distracted and really worried. "I'll go down in a few minutes."

"Cool. Listen, do you mind if I take the car?" Darrel asked.

"Sure, go ahead," Kenya answered, stowing her garbage can back in its place. She smacked her hands together, satisfied with a job well done. She was feeling better already. Mark had been eradicated from her room, and now she was thinking she might actually look Scott up. Aimee was right. There was no use in ruining her life because of what Mark had done. He was not representative of all men.

"So," she said, kneeling down and starting to refill her hatbox with her non-Mark memorabilia, "where are you taking Courtney tonight?"

"I'm heading out for a little late snack at the Half

Café," Darrel said, referring to one of Oak Hills High School's favorite hangouts. "But I'm not going with Courtney. I'm going with Jenn."

"*What?*" Kenya yelled. "When did you and Courtney break up? And why didn't I know about it?"

"You and Courtney were, like, Oak Hills' most perfect couple," Aimee said mournfully. She looked devastated, as if this breakup had shattered her faith in true love forever.

"Calm down, ladies!" Darrel grinned. "Court and I didn't break up. I'm just testing the waters, that's all. Scoping out the other fish."

Something inside Kenya snapped, and her knees turned to instant jelly. She almost crumbled to the floor—almost. A frighteningly strong rush of anger welled up inside her. She reached forward and grabbed an overstuffed pillow from her bed and hurled it at her brother with all the strength she could muster.

"Get out!" she screamed, nearly out of control. She couldn't believe it! Her own brother! Cheating on Courtney Madden—only the coolest person on the planet. She picked up a damp towel from the floor and whipped it in Darrel's direction. Aimee took a step toward the wall, away from Kenya's warpath.

Darrel backed away from the door, a look of sheer terror on his face.

Kenya stalked toward him.

"Chill out, Kenya!" he exclaimed.

"Get out of here, *now!*" Kenya howled again, slamming the door in his face. The frames on Kenya's bedroom wall shook, and a plastic Mickey

Mouse figurine fell off the edge of her desk.

"Okay, okay," she heard Darrel mutter from the other side of the door. "Crazy women."

Kenya leaned back against the closed door and took a deep breath, laying her palms flat against the smooth surface. Then she turned and glared at Aimee.

"Just because Mark and Darrel are both lying cheats doesn't mean—" her friend started.

"Forget it, Aimee," Kenya said tersely. "I am done with guys."

After Aimee left, Kenya pulled the fake ring off her finger and tossed it into the back of her jewelry box. Maybe she'd be able to look at it fondly one day—but not for a long, *long* time. She plodded downstairs with her garbage can, intending to get the rest of the Mark trash out of the house as quickly as possible. As she started out the front door she noticed a weak light coming from the living room.

Mom! I totally forgot about her again! Kenya walked into the living room and found her mother curled up on the couch with a copy of *Newsweek* open in her lap. Her hair was tied back in a ponytail, and she had her reading glasses perched on the end of her nose. The TV screen was blank. *At least she's back to normal,* Kenya thought.

"Hey, Mom," she said quietly.

"Hi, honey," her mom said casually, looking up with a fake smile. Kenya could tell her mom was dying for information. The problem was, as much as Kenya wanted to tell her mom all about what had happened that afternoon—as she usually would—she really didn't feel like talking about it anymore.

"Listen, Mom," Kenya began, settling on the edge of her father's "TV chair," a comfy leather thing that was so huge it really should have been called a love seat. "Mark and I broke up today."

"Oh, Kenya," her mom said, sitting up and leaning forward. "I'm so sorry."

"I'm not," Kenya told her matter-of-factly.

"You're not?" Her mom knitted her brow. "But wasn't today your anniversary?"

"Yeah, it was," Kenya said. She felt a little pang of sadness but pushed it away before it had time to grow. "And Mark seemed to think that cheating on me would be an appropriate present."

Her mother drew in a sharp breath and her brown eyes flashed. "Why, that little—"

"Mom, Mom!" Kenya said with a laugh. "Calm down!" She always found it funny and a bit disconcerting when her mom got riled up. She was a grade-school teacher but never ever raised her voice—not even when little Willie Pandalfo had dumped an entire bottle of red paint on her new white dress *on purpose*.

"I'm okay," Kenya said, putting her hand on the blanket over her mom's knee. "At least I found out now what he's really like. I mean, I could've gone out with him for a lot longer without ever seeing his true colors." Kenya paused, totally baffled and impressed by how mature she sounded. *It's unbelievable the things you'll say when you just want to go to bed,* Kenya thought. Her attitude seemed to have the desired effect. Her mom was really smiling now.

"I'm proud of you, hon." She leaned over to touch Kenya's cheek. Then she got up and started folding her afghan. "All men are pigs anyway."

Kenya's eyebrows rose. "I'm sure Dad would be interested to hear that you feel that way," Kenya said, standing up and grabbing her garbage can.

Her mom laughed. "Oh, he *knows* I feel that way. And he agrees with me."

Kenya shook her head at her mom's silliness. But when her mom opened her arms for a hug, Kenya fell into them gratefully. Somehow, a hug from her mom cured everything, at least for a few minutes.

"What's this?" Kenya's mom asked, gesturing at the trash can as they broke apart.

"Mark memories," Kenya explained.

"Good for you," her mom said, rubbing her back. "Out of sight, out of mind."

"Yeah." Kenya sighed, wondering how long this strange, heavy, numb feeling was going to last. "I sure hope so."

Five

THE NEXT DAY after school, Kenya bounded into the locker room, eager to get changed and head out onto the volleyball court. Immersing herself in a game always made her forget about anything stressful. After the day she'd had yesterday, some total exertion and a major sweat were exactly the forms of athletic therapy she needed.

She leaped over the wooden bench that ran down the length of a bank of lockers and flung her backpack against the row of metal doors with a bang. The amount of nervous energy she had built up thinking about Scott, Mark, and the pixie girl was amazing, and Kenya was practically bouncing as she threw open the door of locker number forty-four. She glanced inside and then slammed the door shut almost instantly.

"What's the matter?" Kenya's friend and teammate Monica Thomas asked. She had entered the locker room just in time to catch the pained look on Kenya's face. Monica slipped off her backpack and reached over to twist the dial on her lock.

"Oh, nothing major," Kenya answered with a sigh. "Just the same thing that's been wrong all day."

Monica shot a questioning glance in Kenya's direction as she reached into her own locker and began to pull out her uniform and pads.

"It's this," Kenya said, flinging the locker door open again with a clang and yanking out a rumpled garment. She shook it out and held it up for Monica to see. It was a gold-colored T-shirt with burgundy block letters that read Taffe Academy.

Monica's eyebrows knitted in confusion. "Isn't that the school your boyfriend goes to?" she asked, pulling her brown-and-white jersey over her head and lifting her thick, curly black hair out of the collar.

"*Ex*-boyfriend," Kenya amended. She crumpled the shirt up into a ball and chucked it into a large garbage can.

"*What?*" Monica shrieked. A couple of other players stopped in their tracks as they entered the locker room. They looked at Monica in disdain.

"Keep it down, rookie," Diana Waters said with a sneer. Diana was Kenya's cocaptain, and while she was an outstanding volleyball player, she was well known for her less-than-sunny attitude.

"Back off, Di," Kenya retorted in her most menacing tone, fixing Diana with a glare. Diana shrugged and continued on toward her own locker, shooting another withering look at Monica and tossing her long red hair over her shoulders. When she and her cohorts had disappeared behind a wall of lockers, Kenya heard a round of giggles float through the room.

A lot of girls on the team, especially seniors like Diana, enjoyed giving Monica a hard time—she was the only sophomore on varsity that year. The rest of the girls had been forced to wait until they were at least juniors, some even seniors, to play varsity. Everyone except Kenya, that is. Because she'd seen varsity court time when she was a freshman, she had been ostracized even more completely than Monica was now. She had had to prove herself on the court, and it had taken some time until her teammates accepted her into their ranks. Since she knew how it felt to be an outsider, she had decided to take Monica under her wing. It was also an added bonus that Monica seemed to worship the ground Kenya walked on.

"Thanks, Kenya." Monica smiled gratefully and pulled her knee pads up over her feet, resting them around her ankles.

"That's okay," Kenya answered. She straightened her jersey and began pulling the backs off her earrings. "I just wish I could figure out whatever happened to team spirit."

"Well, it's not like it's hurting my game at all," Monica said with a disappointed tone. "I never get to play anyway."

"Don't worry. We'll get you out there by the end of the season. And once they see how poised and powerful you are in a game situation, they'll chill out." Kenya patted Monica on the back.

"I hope so, but—*hey!*" Monica stopped Kenya, who was retreating toward the bathroom. "You're not getting away that easily just because you defended my honor. What's all this about an ex-boyfriend?"

Kenya walked back to her locker and dropped onto the bench in front of it. She jammed her foot into her sneaker and wiggled her toes to the front of the shoe. She had hoped Monica would forget about Mark so she wouldn't have to explain it all over again.

"It's kind of a long story," Kenya began. "Let's just say I found out the hard way that I have completely wasted the last year of my life." She yanked at her laces, and they made a zipping sound as if to emphasize her point.

"I'm so sorry, Kenya." Monica sat down next to her and rested her hand lightly on Kenya's shoulder. Her dark brown eyes were wide with concern.

"I'm okay with it," Kenya said in a perky voice that even she didn't believe. "I mean, I'm more angry than depressed, which is good. But I think I would be *totally* fine if I hadn't been reminded of the jerk all day." She stood up and slammed her locker shut. "We don't even go to the same school, but everywhere I look there's some other stupid little thing that reminds me of him." Kenya was pacing now. "First, there was that huge sign in the lobby for the debate team sign-ups. Then the birthday card he gave me was still taped inside my locker. And all those little hearts with his name in them that I actually drew all over my notebooks. Ugh!"

"It's only natural, though, right?" Monica said. She stood and pulled her rings off, placing them on the shelf inside her locker. "I mean, you were together for a whole year. There'll probably be a lot of things that spark little memories. But pretty soon it will start to fade."

"I know you're right," Kenya agreed. "But get this. This is the reason I *know* someone's out to get me. Would you believe the drama department has decided to do *The Music Man*? I mean, come *on!*"

"You lost me," Monica said. "What does *The Music Man* have to do with anything?"

Kenya let out a snort of laughter. "Just that that's the play Mark had the lead in a couple of months ago."

"Well, you have to look on the bright side," Monica said.

"And that would be . . . ?"

"All this aggression will come in handy on the volleyball court," Monica told her. She quickly twisted her hair through a scrunchie and grabbed Kenya's shoulder, rotating her toward the door to the gym.

Kenya heard the sounds of rubber soles squeaking and leather volleyballs smacking against the boards as the teams started to warm up. The tingle of excitement she always felt before a big match surrounded her now like a welcome blanket. Pumped up by a rush of adrenaline, Kenya smiled and hurried toward the gym.

"The Terminator is back," Monica said with satisfaction.

"Goooooooooooooooo Hills!"

The bleachers erupted with applause and cheers

63

as the team broke out of the huddle and burst onto the court. Kenya took the serving position and bounced the ball a few times in front of her. The Oak Hills Mustangs were playing their archrivals, the Maybury Wildcats. Both teams were headed for the playoffs, and the tension in the gymnasium was running high. Kenya glanced at the bench and caught Coach Harrington's eye. He nodded once and Kenya could see the total confidence in his eyes. She nodded back and smiled almost imperceptibly. It was good to know he had faith in the team.

Kenya glared at the Wildcats, making sure she studied each familiar face before she hurled the ball into the air for her serve. They had played this team so many times in the past, she could practically recite their stats.

Whack!

She slammed the ball over the net and into the floor on the Wildcats' side of the court.

"Ace!" Diana shouted triumphantly.

Erin Conor, the team's middle hitter, came over and clapped Kenya on the back as the Oak Hills spectators cheered. Kenya felt another surge of energy. They were off to a promising start.

The ref bounced the ball back to Kenya and she picked it up, resting her fingertips on it for a moment. "One serving zero!" she shouted. She tossed the ball up and pulled her arm back.

Whack!

The other team kept the ball in play, and Kenya felt her teammates spring into position around her. She bent her knees and shifted her weight back and forth, keeping herself ready to pounce in any direction. Kenya followed the ball with her eyes as her opponents passed it two times and then sent it flying over the net. The ball came right at her and she crouched down, passing it easily to a teammate.

"Outside! Outside!" Diana yelled. She jumped up and spiked the ball. It whizzed past the Wildcats players and slammed into the floor.

Kenya reached over and smacked Erin's outstretched hand, then hooked Diana's fingers with her own, pulling back to make a snapping sound.

Piece of cake, Kenya thought, the ball bouncing her way for the next serve.

After possession had turned over a few times, Kenya rotated into her prime position: right in front of the net on the left side of the court. She was an ace outside hitter, and she loved this position because it gave her the opportunity to make the most kills.

"Five serving eleven!" the Wildcats' server yelled. She was an extremely tall and wiry girl named Lee who had scored four of their five points. She leaned back and smashed the ball, letting out a short grunt as her arm flew forward.

It was a low serve and it was heading straight to Kenya. It cleared the net by an inch—an easy block. Kenya reached up and tapped the ball with a flick of her wrist. The ball fell almost straight down on the opponents' side and the Wildcats' middle hitter tipped it, sending it flying back under the net. The girl pushed herself off the floor and growled at Kenya.

Kenya laughed and threw her hands up. "I'm scared," she said sarcastically. Then she watched Erin run a hand over her short blond hair as she surveyed the other team before serving. Kenya knew her teammate was looking for an easy mark and trying to fake the Wildcats out. Erin looked directly at Lee in the far left corner and held her gaze. She threw the ball into the air.

Whack!

The serve sailed toward a smallish brunette in the backcourt on the right. She had already proven herself to be the Wildcats' weakest player. She dove for the ball and just barely kept it in play. One of her teammates saved it, and the ball sailed back over the net. Erin crouched down to pass.

"Right here! Right here!" Diana shouted, bouncing up and down on the balls of her feet. Erin angled her arms and executed a perfect bump.

"Outside!" Kenya shouted. Kenya watched Diana go for the set and readied herself to receive the ball. It soared toward her as if in slow motion.

"This is for you, Mark," she said under her breath. Kenya sprang into the air, keeping her eye on the ball. She could picture Mark's grinning face on the lined surface. Kenya smiled wryly as she pulled her hand back and connected with Mark's nose.

She spiked it perfectly, hitting it with such force she almost took off an opponent's face.

"Point!" the ref yelled.

Kenya and Erin high-fived, and Diana grinned in satisfaction. There was nothing better than playing a match when the whole team was on. Especially when you were demolishing your archrivals. Kenya thought she might try that Mark trick again. The effects of this breakup were getting better and better.

"Wow, Kenya," Monica gushed as the players filed off the court after the first game. "I've never seen anybody play like that. What are you on, some kind of new-wave herbal regimen?"

Kenya plopped into one of the metal folding chairs that made up the "bench" and grabbed her water bottle. The Mustangs had won the first game but had to win the best of three to take the match.

"It's all you," Kenya answered. "You're the one who told me to use aggression."

"That's it? Maybe if I break up with somebody, I'll get some court time!"

"Hey! Monica!" a male voice called out.

"Hi, you guys!" Monica waved toward the door, and Kenya looked up.

Two guys in private-school blazers had just walked in and were making their way around the gym to the bleachers. One was tall and well built with scruffy red hair and freckles. The other was even taller and lean with a dark complexion and short, black hair. *A soccer player and a basketball player,* Kenya assessed mentally. *Both cute.*

"Who are they?" she asked Monica.

"Marcus and Josh?" Monica's eyebrows shot up, as if she was surprised that Kenya was interested. "They're just these guys from Lovett Academy who come to the games. They always say they're coming to see me play, but they know just as well as I do that I never will."

Kenya stared at the gym door and felt her mind start to wander. "I wish Scott would come to a game," she said aloud, before she even realized that the thought had popped into her mind.

"Who's Scott?" Monica asked.

"Oh." Kenya snapped to attention. "This guy I met yesterday." She brought the straw of her water bottle to her lips and took a long sip.

"Yesterday?" Monica said with wonder. "Like, before or after you broke up with your boyfriend?"

Kenya laughed. "Why does everyone need to know that?"

"Monica! C'mere!" The girls looked up to see the redheaded guy waving Monica over and smiling.

"You have a couple of minutes. Go talk to them," Kenya suggested, grateful for the opportunity to avoid any more questions. Talking about this relationship stuff just made it seem all the more overwhelming.

Kenya watched Monica trot across the gym floor and noticed a bunch of guys in Wildcats football jackets following her with their eyes. Sucking on her straw, she studied Monica for a moment. She could see why guys fell all over themselves for her. She had a model's body, her ebony complexion was perfectly clear, and her long hair could have been snatched from one of those Pantene commercials. Kenya shook her head and smiled. Those guys Monica was talking to had come to a game that their school wasn't involved in—a game they knew Monica wouldn't play in—just so they could watch her as she sat on the bench.

Suddenly Monica threw her head back and let out a peal of laughter. Kenya watched her friend rest her hand on the redhead's knee and give him a coy smile. He blushed fiercely and grinned back like a doofus. Meanwhile, the tall guy started playing with Monica's ponytail, batting it around like a kitten in an obvious attempt to get her attention.

"Josh!" Monica squealed playfully. "You're so silly!" She reached up and tousled Josh's hair. As soon as Monica turned her back to him, he shot a triumphant look at the redheaded guy.

Kenya smiled. *If flirting were an Olympic event, Monica would be a gold medalist.*

"Huddle up!" Coach Harrington called out.

Kenya hoisted herself out of her seat and trudged over to join her team as they gathered around the coach and his clipboard.

So I'm not the greatest flirt on the planet, but I'm not a troll, she thought, catching her reflection in the window of the gym teacher's office. *Even after a whole volleyball game I still look pretty good. So why isn't Scott here to see me?* "Because you ran screaming from the train like an insane person," she told herself out loud.

"Huh?" Erin asked, turning from the huddle.

Really gotta do something about this talking-to-myself thing. Kenya joined the huddle and looked over at Monica as she ran up and took a spot next to her. Suddenly Kenya was exhausted again. Thinking about guys sure took a lot out of her.

"How's it going, Terminator?" Monica asked.

"I'm done. Stick a fork in me," Kenya whispered.

"What? What happened to the aggression?" Monica hissed.

"I got distracted."

"Well . . . just . . . I don't know, think of someone else who makes you angry," Monica suggested.

Who could make her more angry than Mark? Darrel? Nah. That whole scene the night before was just Darrel being Darrel. Mrs. Conboy *had* sprung a pop quiz on them that afternoon in French class; Kenya tried to remember how nervous she'd been but then realized she was pretty confident that she'd aced it. Nope—that wasn't gonna do it either.

Kenya thought back to the previous afternoon. She pictured herself walking along happily, swinging Mark's flowers back and forth. She imagined what her face must have looked like when she came around the corner and felt her heart plummet down to the bottom of her patent leather loafers.

Then there was that giggle. An annoying, high-pitched giggle that had haunted Kenya the whole time she was wandering around the city. And that hair! Big, curly red hair—hair Mark had brushed his face against.

Who *was* that girl anyway?

But as Kenya put her hand into the middle of the huddle for the cheer, she realized that the girl's identity didn't matter. She felt the adrenaline surge through her again as she sauntered out onto the court.

No, she thought, *it doesn't matter who the pixie girl was at all, as long as I can picture her perky little face on the surface of the ball.*

"I'll be right up, you guys," Kenya called after the team as they headed back to the locker room. They'd swept the Wildcats two games to none, and everyone was chattering in excitement. If they continued to play like this, the division tournament would be a cinch.

Kenya had almost reached the locker room when she realized she had left her water bottle on the sidelines. She ran back to the gym, snatched up the plastic bottle, and jogged back down the hall.

"Nice game, Clarke!" a couple of straggling fans yelled as they pushed through the back exit doors. Kenya started to answer but was startled when something soft hit her in the face.

"What the—" Kenya said, yanking a towel away from her face.

"Yeah. Nice game, Clarke."

Kenya froze at the sound of his voice. She slowly looked up to see Scott standing in the outside doorway, leaning against the frame. He was wearing baggy tan chinos and a pressed white shirt with a brown leather belt and loafers. He looked *fine.* Kenya was suddenly acutely aware of the profuse amount of sweat that was slowly drying on her skin.

"How long have you been here?" Kenya asked, whipping the towel back at him with a smile. A nervous shiver scampered down her spine.

"I caught the last few minutes of the second

game," he answered. "I thought I'd catch the whole third game, but I guess you're too good for that, huh?"

"Sorry to disappoint you," Kenya said. "How'd you know about the match anyway?" She walked over to the water fountain and began to fill her water bottle, attempting to look nonchalant. But her insides were doing gymnastics. Her hands shook as she held the bottle underneath the stream of water.

Scott held up the sports section of the paper. "I *can* read, you know. Were you aware that you're practically a celebrity?" Scott unfolded the paper and held it out to her. There was a large photo of Kenya jumping up for a spike. The caption underneath read, "Kenya Clarke and the Oak Hills Mustangs take on the Maybury Wildcats in a division showdown this afternoon at 4 P.M."

"Some showdown," Kenya said with a shrug. "We whipped their butts."

Scott refolded the paper and stuck it under his arm. "So, Miss I'm-too-cool volleyball goddess, do you think you could lower yourself to my level long enough to grab a pizza?"

Kenya laughed. She was flying high because of the victory and, she had to admit, because Scott actually had come to see her play. Plus he did look drop-dead gorgeous.

"I think I can descend among the commoners for an hour or so," she said. "Just let me go shower and change." Kenya turned around and opened the locker room door. The sounds of triumphant cheers and running water rushed out along with the smell of steam and soap.

"I'll be right here," Scott said, smiling. He sauntered over to the large glass trophy case in the gym lobby.

"Okay. I won't be too long." Kenya let the locker room door close behind her and sighed contentedly, imagining that killer smile.

I didn't say I was done with guys, did I? Nah! I would never say that.

Six

SCOTT LOOKED AT Kenya as they exited the school and stepped out into the sunshine. So far this was going even better than he'd planned. She'd obviously been shocked to see him, but she'd also seemed pleasantly surprised—which he took as a good sign. Maybe this was going to work out after all.

"So, where's your car?" Kenya asked, surveying the almost empty parking lot.

Maybe not.

"I, uh, don't have one," Scott said.

"You don't have a car?" Kenya asked incredulously. "Then how the heck did you get here?"

"I do have a car," Scott clarified. "It's just in the shop. I had a friend drop me off."

"And how were you planning on getting home?" Kenya asked, putting down her backpack and gym bag so that she could put on her red barn jacket.

"I guess I was kinda hoping maybe, uh, you had a car," Scott answered.

"You were pretty confident I was going to say yes, weren't you?" Kenya asked. She slipped her sunglasses on and shouldered her backpack. As she bent down to pick up her gym bag Scott reached over and grabbed it first.

"I wouldn't say I was overconfident," Scott said, adjusting the nylon strap on his shoulder. "I just didn't think that far ahead." *That sounded great,* he chided himself immediately. *Now she probably thinks I'm beyond stupid.*

"Well, you lucked out this time," Kenya told him lightheartedly, pulling a key ring out of the pocket of her jacket and shaking it in Scott's face. He breathed a sigh of relief. If they had been stranded, he was sure, this relationship would have tanked. *Mental note,* Scott thought. *Always provide transportation.*

Kenya started walking down the slight hill toward the parking lot, and Scott fell into step beside her. He couldn't help stealing glances at her out of the corner of his eye. She was so beautiful, and so confident. He had been amazed at her total control on the volleyball court. Watching her play had made him swell with pride. *As if she were my girlfriend,* Scott thought, smiling. *Maybe after today she will be.* Then he could bring all his buddies to her matches, point out the stunning, world-class athlete who was dominating the court, and say, "See that girl who just spiked the ball down her opponent's throat? That's *my* woman."

They had reached Kenya's car—a little blue Saturn—and she opened the driver's-side door and popped the lock. Scott watched Kenya throw her backpack behind the seat and did the same with her gym bag. Then he slid into the passenger seat and reached underneath for the little pull bar that would move the seat back. Right now his knees were practically up his nose.

"How do you fit in this thing?" he asked as Kenya shut her door and stuck the key in the ignition.

"It's not easy," she said. "But you should be able to move back. Here, let me."

She reached down under his bent legs and yanked the adjuster, sending him shooting backward. It wasn't a perfect fit, but he had more room.

"We didn't think much about comfort when we picked the car out," Kenya explained, pulling out of her parking space. "It's my fault, actually. I wanted a sports car, and I whined until my brother agreed. He wanted a truck."

"You have a brother?" Scott asked. He shifted in his seat and pushed his feet against the front of the car under the dashboard.

"Yeah. He's a year older than me and he's a major pain." Kenya laughed, downshifting as she took a right turn. "But he does always let me have the car on game day, so I don't have to worry about getting a ride."

Kenya pulled the car to a stop at a red light and shifted into neutral. She drummed her fingers on

76

the steering wheel as she waited for the light to change. *She never stops moving,* Scott thought.

The light turned green and Kenya shifted the car into first and then second with a smooth flick of her wrist. *And she drives a stick better than I do,* he noted.

"Wait a minute," Kenya said suddenly as she came to a four-way intersection. "Where are we going?"

Scott blinked. He'd been so intent on studying Kenya, he'd forgotten to let her in on the game plan. "I was thinking we could go to this pizza place over in Harrisburg where I hang out a lot. You just have to make a left here and follow Grand for about ten minutes."

"Sounds good to me," Kenya said, flicking on her left turn signal. "Suddenly I'm starved."

Perfect. Scott leaned back in his seat and sighed with contentment. He was glad she had agreed to his plan so easily. Everyone from his school loved to hang out at Marra's because of the cozy velvet booths, great music, and retro atmosphere. Scott was sure to bump into some of his friends, and he couldn't wait until they saw him with Kenya.

There was an unspoken law in Harrisburg that you didn't hang out at Marra's until you were in high school, unless you came with your family on a Sunday night for dinner. Back when Scott was a freshman, the velvet seats and lava lamps had seemed alien to him, but now whenever he came here he felt as though he were coming home.

"Interesting," Kenya remarked. "I've heard this place is cool but I've never been."

"Why not?" Scott asked as he opened the door.

"Because *you* people hang out here," she answered with a superior look.

"Hey! Don't be knockin' my school," Scott said, sticking out his chest as if he were ready to defend his turf.

"Scotty!" Scott turned to find Sylvia, the young, hip, widely adored manager of Marra's, coming their way with two menus tucked in the crook of her arm. Sylvia had taken over the restaurant from her dad when she graduated from business school. She was wearing her trademark long flowered skirt, and her thick auburn hair was pulled back in a bun. Sylvia was petite and beautiful and never wore any makeup. Half the guys at Scott's school wanted her.

"A new lady, I see," Sylvia said, her eyes sparkling.

"Sylvia, I'd like you to meet Kenya. She goes to Oak Hills."

"Well, we won't hold it against you." Sylvia held out her free hand, and Kenya shook it with a warm smile.

"I appreciate it," Kenya said.

"A cozy table for two?" Sylvia asked as she began to weave her way around the colorful round tables set up in the middle of the restaurant. She didn't wait for Scott to answer and chose a booth against the wall, laying the menus out for them. "Enjoy!" Sylvia said with a smile before disappearing through the swinging doors that led into the kitchen.

Scott sat down on the plush, mustard-colored

seat, making sure he was facing the door. That way he could keep an eye out for anyone he knew. Whenever he came here with his friends, the unlucky souls who had their backs to the door always ended up turning around in their seats whenever they heard someone come in. He cracked his menu to gaze at the familiar fare. He didn't really need to look at it, since he always got the same thing.

"Do you know what you want?" Kenya asked.

Scott looked up and was surprised to see that she hadn't even touched her menu.

"Yeah," he answered. "Do you?"

"I eat only one kind of pizza," she explained. A busboy dressed in a purple silk shirt and black jeans leaned over to pour water for them.

"Me too," Scott said, closing his leather-covered menu and pushing it aside on the polished wooden table. "What's your favorite?"

"Guess," Kenya challenged. She took a gulp out of her water glass and munched on some ice.

"Garlic, anchovies, and pepperoni," Scott said without missing a beat.

"Ugh!" Kenya made a disgusted face and stuck out her tongue. "That's nasty. Who would eat that?"

"That's my favorite." Scott smiled. Everyone was always grossed out by his pizza preference.

"I hope you've never expected anyone to kiss you after you've eaten that," Kenya exclaimed, her eyes wide.

Scott felt a hot flush rise to his cheeks. He hadn't really thought about that. "Well, what's your favorite?" Scott asked quickly, attempting to hide his embarrassment.

"Extra sauce and pineapple," Kenya said, as if it were the most normal thing in the world.

"Pineapple?" he repeated. "*That* is a sacrilege."

"It is not! It's awesome," Kenya argued.

"I bet Sylvia doesn't even *have* pineapple," Scott challenged with a grin. "No self-respecting Italian would put that on a pizza."

"I'll bet she does," Kenya said, smiling conspiratorially.

Scott knew what she was thinking. "All right, Clarke," he said. "If Sylvia agrees to put a big old Hawaiian fruit on the world's most perfect food, I'll try it. But she's never gonna put that stuff on a pizza."

"Put what on a pizza?" Sylvia appeared at their table with a pad and pencil ready.

"Go ahead," Scott said to Kenya, leaning back in his seat. "Ask her."

"Can we have a large pizza with half extra sauce and pineapple?" Kenya requested. Sylvia nodded and wrote it down. "The other half your regular, Scotty?" she asked, collecting their menus.

"You mean you *have* pineapple?" Scott asked with surprise.

"Sure," Sylvia answered. "I can't say I agree with it personally, but a lot of people like it, and we aim to please."

Scott swallowed, and his stomach turned. He was actually going to have to eat it now. Kenya must have noticed his face turning green, because she laughed.

80

"So do you want your regular on the other half or not?" Sylvia asked.

"Yes, please," Scott whispered.

Scott reached for his water glass as Sylvia walked away. Kenya was grinning at him with satisfaction. "What's that look for?" he asked, managing a smile. "She did say she didn't agree with it."

"Yeah, well, she doesn't know what she's missing," Kenya told him.

"So anyway," Scott began, eager to change the subject, "what do you think of the place?"

"I think it's great." Kenya smiled as she looked around. "The furniture is really cool."

Scott tried to see a place that was as familiar to him as his bedroom through Kenya's eyes. The round wooden tables in the center of the room had different-colored tabletops. Around them were all different kinds of chairs, from high-backed wooden ones to stools to well-worn armchairs. There was a cozy area in the corner with a couch, two love seats, and a coffee table. A group of people were hanging out there now, and Scott recognized them as sophomores from his school. They had textbooks open on their laps and on the table, but he could tell by their raucous conversation that they weren't studying. He smiled and looked toward the door. Why weren't any of his friends around?

"Here you go!" Sylvia said several minutes later, placing a steaming pie in the middle of the table. She slid a slice of the pineapple half onto a plate and put it in front of Kenya, then leaned over to cut a slice for Scott from his half.

"No, wait!" Kenya said. "He'll be having a slice of mine first."

Sylvia shot him a questioning look, and Scott groaned but nodded.

Feeling slightly ill, he looked down at the concoction Sylvia had put in front of him. There they were, right on the pizza—large pieces of pineapple, partially covered by tons of sauce and melted cheese. "This looks really weird," Scott said, poking at his food with his fork.

"Well, your half smells like two-week-old garbage," Kenya teased, lifting her slice to her mouth. She took a huge bite and chewed, her eyes closing in happiness. After swallowing she took a sip of water. "My compliments to the chef!" she yelled to Sylvia as the manager breezed by.

Then she turned to Scott. "Come on," she said. "It's now or never."

Scott took a deep breath and picked up his piece of the pie. Enough of this wimpy attitude. It was just pizza. He opened his mouth and took a huge bite, stuffing almost half the slice in his mouth. As he bit into a piece of pineapple he felt the juice squirt out and grimaced. This was too strange. But the sweet taste mixed with the tomatoes was actually pretty good. There was no way he was going to let Kenya know that, though. He swallowed and made a face.

"Oh, please!" Kenya exclaimed. "You didn't like it?"

"I've lost all respect for you," Scott said in a mock-serious tone.

"I can't believe you didn't like it." Kenya sounded disappointed. She leaned back in her seat, looking hurt.

"If I tell you I did, will you try a bite of mine?" Scott asked, pushing the pizza platter toward her.

"You did like it!" Kenya sat up. "I knew it!"

"Maybe." Scott shrugged. "But you'll never know until you try mine."

"Fine," Kenya said, laughing. "If you can do it, I can do it."

Scott watched Kenya as she picked up the pizza cutter Sylvia had left behind and pushed it through the crust toward the middle of the pie. She lifted a slice to her nose, sniffing it warily. Her face screwed up in revulsion as she inhaled. She glanced at Scott, pleading with her eyes.

"Oh, no," he said. "Don't try that pouty act on me. Just take a little bite."

"I do not pout," Kenya objected. She opened her mouth and closed her eyes, then took a good-size bite from the end of the piece. Suddenly her eyes flew open and her hand shot out, groping for her water glass. But instead of picking it up, she knocked it over, spilling the cold liquid all over the table and into her own lap. Scott jumped for the napkin dispenser, but Kenya shook her head at him vigorously.

"Just give me your water!" she sputtered.

He handed her his glass and watched as she gulped it down. The busboy appeared, refilling her glass, and she promptly downed that as well. Scott waited until she swallowed the last drop and put her glass down. Then he burst out laughing.

"Y-Y-You should have s-s-seen your face!" he choked between laughs, pointing at Kenya as she glared at him.

"It's not funny," she said. But he could tell there was a laugh hiding under her voice.

"Yes, it is," he said, replaying her reaction in his mind. He saw the corners of her mouth twitching as she struggled to keep from smiling.

Suddenly she gave up and they both burst out laughing at the same time. Sylvia came over with two towels. She used one to clean up the mess on the table and placed the other one on the bench next to Kenya. They both continued to laugh while she worked, but stopped to look at her guiltily when she was done.

"Kids!" Sylvia said with a shrug before walking away.

Scott and Kenya exploded with laughter all over again.

Finally Scott got control of himself and watched Kenya as she subsided to a giggle. There she was, sitting in a puddle of water, with what was to her a very unpleasant aftertaste in her mouth—and she was laughing. This girl was amazing.

She quieted down and looked back at him, cocking her head to rest her cheek on her hand. They stared at each other for a minute, smiling. Scott could feel his heart pounding in his ears and all the way down to his toes.

Kenya was the first one to break the spell. "I'd better get cleaned up."

"I'm really sorry," Scott said as she stood.

"Don't worry about it," Kenya told him with a wave of her hand. "I have some clean sweatpants in my gym bag. I'll just go grab them out of the car." She headed for the door but stopped when she got halfway across the room and turned around. "Do not even *think* about touching that pineapple," she said. Scott just smiled and waved.

He settled back in his seat and grabbed a slice from his side. He was extremely psyched about how well things were going. His whole day had been spent debating whether or not to come find her. In English lit, when Mrs. Bloom had asked the class to make a list of light and dark imagery in *The Scarlet Letter,* he had made a list of pros and cons of getting together with Kenya. The con side was mostly filled with ways that having a girlfriend would complicate his life, while the pros were filled with details about how great Kenya was. But since he had realized in the darkroom the night before that *not* being with Kenya was going to complicate his life anyway, the answer was pretty clear. He would have to find her and make her his or else he'd flunk out of school and never get any work done in the darkroom again.

And she was so incredible. He couldn't believe she had spilled an entire glass of water on her jeans and hadn't flipped out. She hadn't run screeching to the bathroom or blamed him for the accident. She'd actually laughed it off. Scott shook his head in wonder as he started in on his second slice. Kenya was completely different from any other girl he had ever dated. Completely different from any other girl in his school. Completely different from—

"Hi, Scott!"

Emma Hunt.

Scott swallowed nervously as Emma and her two best friends, Wendy Stewart and Renee Barsa, sauntered over to his table. He had known Emma since he was little, and they shared a lot of the same friends. They had always hung out together, but ever since he had taken her to the winter formal, Emma had been flirting with him. Everyone at Harrisburg High thought he was an idiot for passing up a chance with Emma Hunt—she was gorgeous and popular and sweet and smart. *And I'm not in the least bit interested in her,* Scott thought.

Emma sat down on the bench next to Scott, and he inched closer to the wall. She tossed her dark wavy hair over one shoulder and blinked at him with her heavily made-up lashes. The thick, flowery scent of her perfume mixed with the smell of anchovies and garlic. Scott put his slice back on his plate, his appetite beginning to vanish.

"Mind if we join you?" Wendy asked. She slid into the space Kenya had just vacated before he had a chance to answer.

"Actually," Scott began, "I'm sort of —"

"What're you doing here alone?" Renee asked, raising her eyebrows as she sat down next to Wendy.

"Nothing. I mean, I'm not exactly alone—"

"So," Emma began, cutting him off, "are we still on for tonight?" She reached in front of him and picked a piece of pepperoni off his slice between two perfectly manicured fingernails.

"Tonight?" Scott asked. He shot a look toward the door, waiting for Kenya to come back inside and freak. Having three girls hovering around him the moment she walked away would not look good.

"You said you'd help me with geometry, remember?" Emma whined.

Scott stopped himself from rolling his eyes. Before she'd become interested in him, Emma had been a lot easier to get along with. She was usually laid back and cool, but when she liked a guy—as she clearly liked Scott now—she could be totally overbearing. "Of course I remember," he answered, glancing at his watch. Was it seven o'clock already? "I'll call you as soon as I get home," he told Emma, begging silently, *Please go away now.*

Instead, Emma reached both hands around his neck and started playing with his collar. "Your shirt's all messed up," she said in a flirtatious voice.

Just then Kenya walked through the door, gray sweatpants in hand, and stopped short in front of the register.

Scott caught her eye and watched in dismay as her face fell. Then her eyes became totally cold and distant and the rest of her expression hardened. She walked toward him stiffly. Emma was still fiddling with his collar and giggling. He shrugged her off with a violent jerk of his arm. *Maybe I can still salvage this,* Scott thought. *Kenya's a reasonable person.*

"Hey, Kenya, I'd like you to meet—" Scott began.

"My pleasure," Kenya cut him off. She walked around the end of the table and snatched up her purse from the bench. Then, without even looking at Scott, she turned back toward the door.

"You're leaving?" Scott asked incredulously. This was a little harsh, wasn't it?

Kenya just kept walking, and Emma was blocking his way out of the booth. He looked at her in desperation. She smiled back.

"Emma, could you excuse me, please?" he asked, trying to sound polite. It came out as more of a snarl.

She slid out of the seat and he jumped up, knocking the table with his knee and causing the dishes to jump.

"Rude much?" he heard Emma mutter as he followed Kenya outside.

She was getting into her car. Scott ran over to the window and bent down. "You didn't even finish eating," Scott said, trying to restore some kind of normalcy to the situation. He really didn't see what the big deal was. If she'd give him one second to explain, she would see she was overreacting. "Come on. Come back inside. They're just friends and they weren't staying."

"Hey, it's no big deal," Kenya said, slipping on her sunglasses without looking at him. "I just realized I have to go."

"Kenya, what's the matter?" Scott asked in what he thought was a soothing voice.

"Nothing!" she practically shouted. Startled, Scott restrained himself from jumping back. What was going on with her? There had to be more going on here than just being upset about Emma and her friends.

"Please, Scott," she said softly, turning her face toward his. "Please just let me go," she said. Her hands shook.

Scott looked at her for another moment, searching for some kind of reason to explain why she had transformed so abruptly from carefree Kenya into this cold person behind the wheel of the car. A tear slid down her cheek.

"Okay," he said finally. He stood and backed up a little to let her pull out of the space. "I've entered the Twilight Zone," he said out loud as he watched her drive off.

He walked back over to Marra's and leaned up against the outside wall, trying to figure out what had just happened. Sure, he knew that thing with Emma had looked bad, but Kenya's over-the-top reaction hardly seemed to fit with what he knew of her so far. A girl who hardly minded a cup of water in her lap didn't seem the type to bolt from a slightly suspicious scene without at least waiting for an explanation. *There has to be more to it,* Scott thought again. *But what?*

"Forget it!" he said out loud. He suddenly realized his palms were sweating, and he wiped them on his pants. "If you didn't think you could deal with a girlfriend, try dealing with a girlfriend who runs out crying at the end of every date," he muttered under his breath. He walked over and held the door open for a group of freshmen girls who were going inside.

"Hey, my man!"

Scott let the door close in front of him and turned to see Jeff striding across the parking lot toward the restaurant, a huge grin on his face. He had just come from track practice and was freshly showered, wearing a clean white T-shirt and cotton shorts. Typically, a couple of the freshman girls turned around to drool through the restaurant window.

"What's up?" Scott said halfheartedly, reaching out to slap hands with Jeff.

"Not much," Jeff said. "I just figured I'd stop by and grab some grub before hittin' the books. Who're you here with?"

Scott grimaced. "I *was* here with Kenya, but she bailed." Scott shrugged and tried not to sound as disappointed and confused as he felt.

"Bailed? You made her up, didn't you?" Jeff joked, his green eyes sparkling. "No girl would ever fall for you, Hutson. Just give it up."

"Whatever, Pierce," Scott shot back with a small smile. "Maybe she heard you were comin' and that's why she sprinted to her car."

As Jeff laughed, Scott studied his friend. It might be a good thing that Kenya had left before Jeff showed up. *She'd probably forget about me instantaneously,* Scott thought. From what his female friends told him, Jeff was "the finest guy alive." Scott, of course, had no opinion on this. But as he eyed his best friend now, he could sort of see why women would go for him. He had jade green eyes, chocolate brown skin, and a contagious smile. Plus he was on the football and track teams, which always scored points with the ladies.

"No, really, man," Jeff said, containing his laughter. "Why'd she leave?"

"Long story," Scott answered, following his friend into Marra's. "But I'll tell you all about if you try a piece of pineapple pizza."

"*Pineapple?*" Jeff repeated, turning to look at Scott with a bewildered expression.

"Hey, it was her idea," Scott told him as he led the way back to the table. He was relieved when he noticed that Emma, Wendy, and Renee had moved to a booth in the back corner.

Jeff slid into Scott's booth and grimaced as he studied the pie. The cheese had gotten cold and was starting to congeal over the slices of fruit. "This girl of yours must be insane," Jeff declared, grabbing a slice from Scott's half of the pizza.

Scott took a sip of water. After witnessing Kenya's bizarre emotional shifts, Scott was beginning to wonder about her sanity himself.

Seven

KENYA ROLLED ONTO her back and placed her open chemistry text over her face. She inhaled deeply and let the textbook smell fill her nostrils. *Maybe I can be the first high-school student in the history of the world to actually learn by osmosis,* she thought. "It sure ain't happenin' any other way," Kenya said into the slick pages.

She grabbed the book with both hands and pulled it away, hoisting herself into a sitting position at the same time. Kenya surveyed her room from her queen-size bed. The place was immaculate. There wasn't a pair of dirty jeans, an open Snapple bottle, or a stray piece of jewelry in sight. Earlier, Kenya had stashed everything in its proper place, figuring that maybe her clutter was distracting her from studying. Kenya sighed and straightened her throw pillows for the umpteenth time. She knew, of course, that it wasn't her surroundings that were bothering her. It was Scott.

It had been an entire week since the fiasco at Marra's and she hadn't heard from him. Not that she expected to. *Only a lunatic would call a person who ran out on him in tears two days in a row,* Kenya thought. *I mean, consider this logically. Do you really want to date the kind of person who would actually date you after your bizarre outbursts?*

Kenya rolled out of her bed and crossed the room to her window seat. The huge window looked out over her backyard and the woods beyond. The sun was just setting behind the budding trees, turning the sky a million shades of pink, from subtle to brilliant. Kenya picked up the tattered stuffed lamb that she'd had since her third birthday and held it against her chest.

Leaning back against the wall, Kenya lifted her legs up onto the softly cushioned seat and stretched out. She brought Lamby up to her face and rested her chin on the stuffed animal's soft head, staring out at the sky.

She couldn't believe the way she'd acted around Scott. *I used to pride myself on being a strong person,* Kenya thought, exhaling slowly. *Did Mark really take that away from me?*

Mark hadn't called either, and in some ways, Kenya was glad. She couldn't imagine actually hearing his deep baritone voice blubbering through some lame, half-baked excuse. She almost thought more of him for *not* calling. He knew he'd been caught. Why bother lowering himself even further, and insulting Kenya's intelligence, by trying to make her believe some stupid story?

"Well, you could've at least called to give me the chance to yell at you," Kenya said to the window. "Now *that* would have been truly chivalrous."

Kenya stood and replaced Lamby on the window seat. She walked over to her antique bureau and pulled out her favorite article of clothing in all the world—a huge, cozy, heather gray sweatshirt, size XXL, with UCLA scrawled across the front in gold letters. The cuffs of the sleeves were worn and the shirt was broken in to perfection. Kenya smiled for a moment, remembering a night at the lake the previous summer when Mark had tried to steal the shirt from her and she had tackled him into the freezing cold water.

What am I thinking? Kenya shook her head to banish the images of her ex. She shouldn't be having any happy thoughts about that pixie girl–loving pain in the butt.

No more Mark. No more Scott. No more love, period.

This way I won't get hurt and I will avoid being thrown out of every public establishment in town for shameless weeping. Kenya yanked the sweatshirt over her head and tugged it down to her thighs.

She stood in the center of her bedroom and looked at her chem book with an overwhelming feeling of irritation. It was lying on her bedspread, opened to the problems page, which was obviously mocking her. She *really* didn't want to study right now.

"Kenya!" Her father's voice boomed up from the living room. "You have a visitor!"

Visitor? But she hadn't even heard the doorbell ring. *Who cares?* she thought. *I'm saved!*

Kenya bolted from her room and padded down the carpeted stairs in her sock-clad feet. *What would I do without Aimee?* she thought. Their best-friend telepathy thing must have kicked in and alerted Aimee to Kenya's dire need for a study break.

"Perfect timing," Kenya sang as she swung around the corner into the foyer. But when she saw who was standing there, her eyes widened in shock. "Scott?"

Kenya tried to pull to a stop, but her socks slid on the vinyl flooring. She teetered for a moment and almost hit the floor. In desperation she groped for the doorjamb with her hand, finally clutching the wall for support.

"Hi," Scott said with a smile. "That was rather graceful." He pulled his hand from behind his back and offered her a bouquet of a dozen beautiful yellow roses adorned with baby's breath.

Kenya gasped. "What are these for?" she asked, bringing the flowers to her face and drinking in their wonderful scent.

"The one-week anniversary of our second disastrous unofficial date," Scott said in a matter-of-fact tone.

Kenya felt her cheeks burn and fixed her eyes on his shoes—a very clean pair of Docksides. "They weren't disastrous," Kenya told him, continuing to stare at his feet.

"Really?" he asked. "I thought any afternoon that ended in tears could pretty much be ruled a failure. I'm

95

not sure, but I think I read that in *GQ* or something."

Kenya looked up at his face, expecting to see disappointment or possibly even mocking in his expression. Instead, he looked confused, concerned, and hopeful. Her heart warmed, her spirits rising a little.

"How'd you find me?" Kenya asked, realizing she hadn't given him her address.

"It was pretty simple, actually." Scott shoved his hands into the pockets of his blue cotton jacket and flashed a self-satisfied grin. "Oak Hills is a small town. There're actually only two Clarkes in the phone book, and the little old white guy at twenty-two Lafayette kindly informed me that Kenya was a country in Africa—right before he slammed the door in my face."

Kenya laughed. "So by process of elimination . . ."

"I ended up here," Scott finished.

"Good old forty-nine Mine Street," Kenya said, reaching out to pat the wood-paneled wall. "Where the residents know that Kenya is much more than a country in Africa."

"You can say that again," Scott said with a sly smile.

"We have to talk," she said, making a sudden decision. If Scott was devoted enough to track her down through the phone book *and* risk braving her insanity a third time *and* bring her roses, he deserved the truth. Kenya placed the flowers on the foyer table and stuffed her feet into a pair of Keds. For the first time in her life, she was grateful for her family's leave-your-shoes-by-the-door rule. Kenya clasped Scott's wrist and swung open the front door.

"Where are we going?" he asked as she pulled him out onto the steps.

Instead of answering, Kenya yelled inside to her father, "Dad! I'm going for a walk!" Her dad appeared in the doorway, his muscular, six-foot-six-inch frame nearly filling the entire space. He had a stern look on his face that Kenya knew was forced—her father was an extremely easygoing parent. "You met Scott at the door, right, Daddy?" she asked.

"Sure," her father answered, crossing his arms in front of his plaid-flannel-clad chest. "Just don't keep her out too long, son," he said in a voice to match his expression.

Kenya almost laughed. But Scott bought the act.

"Of course not, sir," he said.

Kenya began to lead Scott across the plush lawn to the street.

"Honey?" her father called after her. Kenya turned to look at her dad as Scott squatted to tie his shoelace.

"He's cute," her father mouthed, batting his eyelashes comically. Kenya rolled her eyes.

"Thanks, Dad!" she said with a laugh. Then she grabbed Scott by the arm and started pulling him toward the sidewalk.

"Why are we going for a walk?" Scott asked.

"I can't think straight when I'm in the same house with my chemistry book."

Scott shot her his little brow-crease look. Kenya grinned. *Damn, I love that.*

★   ★   ★

Ten minutes later, Kenya and Scott were strolling side by side around the red clay track behind Oak Hills Middle School. Kenya lived about a block away from her old school and often came up here to think when she was confused or depressed. It took her back to a time when everything was much simpler. The place had a calming effect on her.

Kenya had just finished telling Scott about her breakup with Mark. She had left out a few details—one redheaded giggly detail in particular. The fact that Mark had cheated on her and had completely fooled her into thinking he was faithful was beyond embarrassing for Kenya. So, she had simply told Scott that Mark had royally messed up their anniversary and left it at that. But everything else she had told him was on the line, including the part about being shocked by the breakup.

"I just think I need to take things slowly, you know?" Kenya said, staring at the ground as she spoke. "I mean, he really hurt me."

"I can tell," Scott said quietly.

"I'm really not this emotional normally," Kenya asserted, bending down to pluck a fluffy dandelion from the grass in the center of the track oval. She was so nervous, she needed something to fiddle with. "I mean, I feel like my life has become one big sappy episode of *Days of Our Lives*."

Scott cracked a smile, and she let out a little sigh of relief.

"So, are you still in love with this guy?" he asked suddenly.

Kenya was a little taken aback by the question. It was so abrupt and to the point. But she had to admit she hadn't really thought about it. Love . . . Mark. She twirled the dandelion between two fingers. Those two words didn't belong in the same sentence. In fact, the mere thought of linking them together was an affront to decent sentences everywhere.

"No," she said slowly. Then she considered for a moment. "In fact, I'm not sure I ever really was in love with him." *After all,* she added to herself, *you obviously didn't even know him.*

"So I definitely didn't do anything wrong," Scott prodded.

Kenya shook her head. "It was all him," she answered, silently cursing Mark again. She tossed the flower aside and watched as it hit the pavement and all the little seeds took flight. It was getting chilly out, and Kenya shivered, pulling her hands up inside the arms of her sweatshirt. A light breeze skittered by, and she felt goose bumps popping up on her skin.

Scott reached out and rubbed his hands up and down her arms, and she warmed instantly, surprised by his gesture. But a moment later he frowned and yanked his hands away. She watched in dismay as he folded his arms across his chest and tucked his hands beneath his elbows.

"Listen," he said, his voice suddenly distant. "You said you need to take things slow, so I understand if you need some time alone. Backing off is not a problem, if that's what you want me to do."

Kenya struggled to find the words she wanted to

say. What was she feeling? A couple of days earlier, all she'd wanted to do was protect herself. But now she was thinking that maybe she had it all backward. Maybe Scott could protect her.

Scott must have taken her prolonged silence as a bad sign.

"I guess I'd better go," he said in a flat voice, turning away. Kenya watched his retreating back for a moment, desperate to find a way to make him understand where she was coming from.

"Don't go!" she blurted out. *Lame,* she thought. But it did have the desired effect. Scott turned around and raised his eyebrows hopefully.

"Look," Kenya began, closing the distance between them. "I may be totally confused and prone to sudden outbursts of emotion, but I do know one thing for sure."

"What's that?" Scott asked.

Kenya reached up and placed her hands on his shoulders, being careful not to let her fingers slip out of her sleeves. "I enjoyed every minute of those disastrous unofficial dates," she said, staring into his eyes.

Scott let out a short laugh. "Even the minute when your mouth was filled with garlic, anchovies, and pepperoni?"

"There *was* a major ick factor for a while," Kenya said, scrunching her nose at the memory. "I think I had to brush my teeth forty times before I got the taste out. I probably still stink."

"You smell pretty good to me," Scott said in a husky whisper.

"You think so?" Kenya asked flirtatiously. Her heart pounded as the perfect line popped into her head. *Can I really say that?* she thought. *Sure. Why not?*

"Did you ever find out if you were kissable after eating that concoction?" she asked softly.

Scott's mouth curled up into a wry smile.

He was so close that Kenya could feel his breath on her cheek. It smelled sweet, felt warm, and left a tingly sensation on her skin. *Seems kissable to me,* Kenya thought. Her pulse was racing, and she could feel her skin warming all over her body.

"I had a slice this afternoon," he said, slipping his arms around her waist and pulling her even closer. Kenya felt her goose bumps melt away as his warm jacket shielded her from the breeze. "Are you game?"

Kenya didn't answer. Instead, she slipped her hand around his neck and pulled his lips down to meet hers. As soon as they touched, Kenya caught her breath and an exhilarating yet somehow fuzzy feeling rushed through her, making her light-headed and causing her to swoon slightly. No kiss with Mark—private or not—had ever felt like this. Another shiver ran down her back, but this one had nothing to do with the cold.

Oh, yeah, Kenya thought. *Definitely kissable.*

Eight

SCOTT PULLED HIS black Jeep Wrangler into the spot right next to Kenya's Saturn. It was a perfect Saturday, two days after his perfect first kiss with Kenya. The weather was beautiful, warm enough to spend the whole day outside in a T-shirt without once wishing for a sweater. And that meant only one thing to Scott—it was top-down weather. No matter what reason any Jeep owner ever gave for buying their automobile, there was only one real reason: Driving around with the top down, radio blasting, sunglasses on, the wind in your face, and the sun on your back, you *knew* you were the coolest person on the planet.

Feeling totally pumped, Scott slammed the door behind him and reached into the backseat to grab his black canvas camera bag. When Kenya had called that morning and invited him to the YMCA for a volleyball lesson, Scott had been totally surprised. Every time Kenya opened her mouth, Scott ended up being more and more impressed. Now it turned out that she volunteered to teach volleyball to little kids on Saturday mornings. Was there anything this girl didn't do?

Scott walked into the lobby of the large brick building. The structure was relatively new and still had that fresh, clean, just-constructed smell. His sneakers squeaked on the shiny waxed floor, where a mosaic was worked into the tiles depicting a bunch of kids running hand in hand. Scott followed an arrow painted on the wall that was marked Gymnasium. He knew he should be working on his photography project, and a tiny twinge of guilt popped up in his mind. But Scott pushed the irritating feeling aside as he got close to the gym. He could hear Kenya's voice floating through the doors—Kenya with kids was something he didn't want to miss.

"That's right everybody, pair off," she was saying. He peeked through the slim glass pane in the center of the wooden door and glimpsed a bunch of kids, all eyeing one another nervously.

"Are you guys going to pick your own partners, or am I going to have to do it for you?" Kenya asked in a slightly threatening tone. Scott shook his head and chuckled. He pressed the handle on the door and entered quietly in an attempt to avoid drawing attention to himself. A little girl with blond pigtails glanced in his direction but blinked back up at Kenya when she started to call out names.

Scott silently slipped his camera out of his bag

and crouched on the floor. If there was one thing his father had taught him about being a photographer, it was never to pass up the opportunity to take pictures of kids. They were the most expressive subjects you could find.

"You can't put me with Ian!" the little girl with the pigtails exclaimed, a look of pure astonishment on her face. "He's a *boy*."

Kenya knelt down, and Scott snapped a few pictures. Kenya looked very athletic in her gray spandex shorts and red Nike T-shirt. Even squatting down, she dwarfed the tiny girl. But the little girl didn't seem to notice. Instead she looked absolutely offended.

"You should have thought of that when I asked you to pick partners, Stephanie," Kenya told her lightly. "Besides"—she leaned in toward Stephanie's tiny ear and spoke in a hushed, conspiratorial tone—"Ian's not very good. He needs your help. You know you're the best setter I've got." Kenya leaned back and looked at Stephanie as if she were desperate.

Stephanie's face beamed. "Don't worry, Ms. Clarke," she said, laying a tiny hand on Kenya's shoulder. "I'll whip him into shape." With that she spun around, pigtails flying, and bounced over to where Ian was waiting with a volleyball tucked under his arm.

Kenya stood up and clapped her hands. "Okay! Let's see those sets!" she yelled. The children all sprang into action, setting volleyballs to their partners.

Scott let out a tiny whistle, and Kenya spun around. Her eyes lit up when she saw him, and

Scott's heart did a somersault as he realized that happy look was for him. Kenya skipped over, planting a light kiss on his cheek.

"Not bad, Ms. Clarke," he said. "Have you ever thought about teaching?"

"Actually, yeah," Kenya answered, grinning. "But after an hour with these little monsters I'm usually reduced to a useless ball of quivering mush, so I don't know how I'd manage an entire day." Kenya reached over and took the camera out of his hands. Scott almost snatched it back, being very protective of his photography equipment. But Kenya handled it carefully, and he relaxed.

"You could teach and coach volleyball," Scott suggested as she turned the lens toward him.

"That's an option," Kenya said, squinting as she held the viewer up to her right eye.

"What're you doing?" Scott asked.

"Taking pictures of the only worthy subject in the room," she answered with a laugh as she squeezed off a few shots.

Scott struck a pose, crossing his arms over his white T-shirt and leaning back against the wall. Two seconds later he started to feel extremely silly. He reached over and grabbed the camera.

"Hey! I was just getting good at that!" Kenya protested.

Scott held the camera out of her grasp. "I think some of your loyal subjects need you," he said, lifting his chin in the direction of the children.

"Is not!" Stephanie yelled.

"Is too!" Ian answered. "Girls don't know anything about superheroes!"

Kenya slumped her shoulders comically. "Back to the grindstone," she mumbled.

"What's the big tragedy this time?" Kenya asked, trudging over to the arguing kids. The two children were facing each other in a standoff, and Kenya knelt down in between them, facing Scott. He adjusted his lens for a close-up and poised himself for the shot.

"He says Wolverine's the best." Stephanie huffed at the indignity of it all.

"She says Storm's the coolest," Ian said, facing Kenya. "Storm's a stupid *girl!*"

Kenya looked up at Scott and rolled her eyes, but her mouth was smiling. Scott laughed and snapped off a few pictures. These kids were cute, but they had no idea what they were talking about. Everyone knew Iceman was the most powerful of the X-Men.

"If you two don't start practicing and stop talking about cartoons, I'm going to tell your parents to stop taping *X-Men* while you're here," Kenya said, picking up the ball from where Stephanie had dropped it and handing it back to Ian. "Besides, everyone knows Jubilee is the best."

Kenya stood and started to walk back toward Scott.

"*Jubilee?*" Stephanie, Ian, and Scott all said in unison.

"But she's not even a real X-Man," Ian protested. Kenya shot a withering look over her shoulder, and Ian bit his lip, took a step back, and set the ball to Stephanie. A few minutes later a couple of parents filtered through the doors and Kenya clapped her hands again.

"Okay, team! Time's up! Grab your stuff and I'll see you next week."

Scott watched in awe as the entire class gathered around Kenya and hugged her bare legs. She patted them on their heads before they turned and ran to the far wall, where their bags and water bottles were waiting. Kenya picked up a stray volleyball and bounced it against the floor like a basketball as she sauntered over to Scott.

"They love you," Scott marveled, placing his camera in his bag.

"They fear me," Kenya corrected him with a sly grin.

"Okay, they do fear you," Scott said. "And I'm beginning to feel the same way myself."

"You should, photo boy." Kenya rocketed the ball toward Scott's chest, and he reached up and caught it with both hands. Kenya arched an eyebrow.

"I have a few moves of my own," Scott said with a modest shrug.

"Well, if you're so great all of a sudden, let's volley a little bit and see what you've got," Kenya challenged.

Scott followed her out onto the full-size volleyball court and took his place on the opposite side of the net. He set the ball over to her, silently praying he would remember the basics he'd been taught in gym class. He knew Kenya was a seasoned pro, and he wanted to at least hold his own against her. Ten minutes later he had miraculously avoided letting the ball hit the floor, and Kenya joined him on his side of the net.

"You know what I think?" she said flirtatiously, snatching the ball away from him and holding it behind her.

"What's that?" he asked, folding his arms. He was not going to give in to her little attempt to goad him into trying to get the ball back.

"I think I should stop going so easy on you."

Okay, maybe he would give in.

Before Kenya could react, Scott pounced. Wrapping his arm around her slim waist, he grabbed for the ball. Kenya let out a little yelp of surprise and the ball went flying out behind her. Scott held her back with one arm as he leaned down and reached out for the ball with his other hand. She twisted out of his grasp and caught his ankle with hers, sending them both tumbling to the ground. Kenya somehow rolled over and grabbed the ball, clutching it against her chest. There was only one thing Scott could do.

"Tickle torture!" he yelled. He always threatened Tracy with that when she wouldn't go to bed or clean up her toys.

Kenya looked up at him, her eyes wide with fear as Scott grabbed her waist and started to tickle. "No! No! No!" she wailed as she wriggled around, laughing. "You can't do this to me!"

"Give up the ball!" he answered, with no intention of letting up until she did exactly that.

"Never!" she yelled.

She is brave, Scott thought as he upped the tickle dosage.

"Ahem!"

Scott and Kenya sprang apart on the floor, turning over into sitting positions to check out their visitor. An extremely tall man with a mustache stood in the doorway. He was wearing a tank top and sweats and held a basketball under his arm. A few other guys were hovering behind him, all looking on with amused expressions.

"I believe we have the gym this hour," the mustached man said. "Unless wrestling practice takes precedence."

Scott and Kenya scrambled to their feet and reached for their bags.

"Sorry," Kenya mumbled. "I didn't know anybody had signed up for this time."

"No problem." The man entered the gym with his friends and put his stuff down against the wall. Scott clasped Kenya's hand as they ducked through the door into the hallway.

"That was so embarrassing!" Kenya gasped once they were out of earshot from the gym.

On impulse, Scott grabbed her around the waist with one arm and pulled her to him. She stared into his eyes and he heard a little gasp catch in her throat. He smiled, leaning in to kiss her. She went slightly limp in his arms and Scott tightened his hold, wrapping his other arm around her back as he deepened his kiss. He loved that he had such a melting effect on her.

As he pulled away he realized that she had that same effect on him. His knees had become jelly, and he leaned back against the wall so she wouldn't notice how weak she made him.

Kenya smiled at him dreamily, a slightly dazed look in her eyes.

"I love you, Kenya," Scott heard himself say.

Suddenly Kenya's eyes clouded over. Scott's heart broke at the sudden shift in her expression.

"I'm sorry," he sputtered. "I . . . I don't even know what I was saying."

"It's okay."

Scott felt numb. She had told him two days before that she had just gotten out of a bad relationship and wanted to take it slow, and now he was pushing her into a serious thing with him. *How could I be so insensitive?* he thought. *Those are probably the last three words she wants to hear from anybody right now.*

"No, it's not okay, Kenya," he said.

She turned and started toward the parking lot, and he followed her, wanting to make things right. He was pretty sure he *was* in love with her, and he wasn't about to lose her because he'd been stupid enough to say it too soon. *I'm the one who didn't want anything complicated, and I just keep making things worse,* Scott scolded himself.

Kenya stopped when she got to the driver's-side door of her car.

"Look," she said. "It *is* okay. I'm fine. Really."

She kissed him quickly on the cheek, then jumped into her car.

Scott leaned back against the Jeep as she started the engine. Kenya looked up and granted him a half smile before pulling away.

Not exactly the reaction you want when you spill your guts to a girl, he thought. *But it's your own darn fault. What were you thinking, Hutson?*

Scott walked around the front of his car and climbed in, placing his bag on the floor next to him. *At least she didn't run off crying this time,* he thought. But as he flicked the radio on and pulled out of his space, Scott had a sinking feeling that even though she hadn't been in tears, after this time she wouldn't want to see him again.

On Monday all the schools in the area had the day off for a teachers' conference. Kenya had decided to take off for the city right after lunch. The coach had told her about this new athletic shop that had a huge volleyball section, and Kenya wanted to check it out.

The little trip was also a convenient way to avoid Scott. She had managed to get out of talking to him the previous day by spending the whole day at Aimee's house watching movies, studying, and eating raw cookie dough. But Monday Aimee was helping her older sister move into her new apartment, so Kenya had had to come up with an alternate plan.

What she hadn't realized when she'd decided to

come find this place was that it was in the same neighborhood as Mark's school. So on top of feeling lost again, she was also a nervous wreck, wondering if she might bump into him. That was the last thing she needed.

Kenya looked around and smoothed her hair back with the palm of her hand. PJ's Italian Restaurant. Hadn't she seen that before? *Oh, who am I kidding?* she thought, pushing up the sleeves of her white cotton sweater. *I will never again come into Chicago when I am in any way distracted by a guy. Or two guys, in this case.*

Kenya pulled the little piece of paper on which she had scribbled Coach Harrington's directions out of the back pocket of her jeans. She glanced at it briefly and then chucked it into a garbage can. She was about to turn around and head back to the el when she realized why she remembered PJ's. It was right around the corner from that spooky flower place.

Figuring that with her terrible sense of direction she was probably wrong, Kenya walked around the corner just to see.

But there it was: Anita's Flowers and Fortunes.

This is just too weird, Kenya thought. *What am I, like, drawn to this place or something?*

Whatever. Kenya didn't believe in all that psychic stuff anyway. But as she started to move away from the tiny shop, she hesitated. The creepy old lady *had* been right about Mark. Maybe Kenya should just go in for a minute and feel the place out again. Maybe the woman had some kind of prediction about Scott. Maybe she could even tell Kenya why she had been so freaked out when Scott had told her he loved her. He was totally perfect. What was her problem? Kenya took a deep breath and pushed through the door, causing the bells to let out an agitated jangle.

"Hello, dear." The little old woman was sitting behind the counter, sipping some tea. Her beady blue eyes were still as cold as ice, even though her voice was sugary sweet.

"Anita, right?" Kenya said in the gruffest voice she could manage. Maybe if she acted belligerent, she could prevent herself from getting all weirded out.

"That's right," the woman responded, smiling. Her eyes softened slightly, as if she appreciated Kenya's new attitude.

"Yeah, well, *Anita,* I was in here a couple of weeks ago and you told me something that really . . . well, something that turned out to be totally right," Kenya finished lamely.

"That's good, dear," Anita said, standing up and lifting her thick white braid over her shoulder. "I'm glad I could be of some service." She picked up her teacup and started to shuffle through an open doorway into a back room. Kenya let out a sigh and followed.

"The truth is, it didn't do me a bit of good," Kenya said. "I still got totally crushed."

Kenya's complaint was cut short as she stood in the doorway. She didn't really know what she had expected to find. Maybe a big round table and lamps

113

covered with glittery scarves and tarot cards and beads and a glass ball or something. But Anita's back room was decorated in a very sparse and bright manner. There was a large, polished blond wood table in the middle of the room with two comfortable-looking armchairs on either side, each upholstered in a pink flowered fabric. Framed art prints hung on the walls, and a tiny tabby cat yawned lazily from its resting place on a high windowsill.

"I can't help people if they don't take my advice," Anita said, turning to face her. "Have a seat."

"What if I don't want to?" Kenya asked, finding it hard to remain defensive in the face of such normalcy.

"You want to," Anita assured her, the sides of her eyes crinkling up as she smiled.

Anita sat down in one of the chairs, and Kenya guiltily slid into the place across from her. She suddenly felt really bad about giving this little old lady a hard time.

"Let me have your hand," Anita said, reaching out her fingers. Her nails were really long—like claws—but her hands were clean and soft-looking.

Kenya hesitated a moment, remembering the cold shock she'd gotten the last time she'd touched Anita. But at least this time she knew what to expect. Besides, maybe it had just been her imagination working overtime because she had been so intimidated by her surroundings. She thrust her hand out across the table.

Anita took Kenya's hand, clasping it within both of hers. The bolt of ice shot through Kenya's arm and she almost snatched her hand away, but Anita's grip was like a vise. Kenya watched, feeling increasingly frightened as Anita closed her eyes and tilted her head back. The old woman's face twitched slightly, and Kenya decided to study the colorful beaded necklace that hung against the woman's plush purple sweater. *Why did I come in here?* Kenya badgered herself. Swallowing was suddenly difficult, and Kenya wished Anita would just let go of her.

"You find it hard to trust," Anita said suddenly, without opening her eyes.

"Maybe," Kenya responded noncommittally. She didn't want to give too much away.

"There is a new relationship and you will not let yourself go," Anita commented. "But this will only hurt you."

"Hurt me?" Kenya exclaimed, suddenly indignant. "The last time I 'let myself go,' as you put it, that's when I got hurt."

"But this boy is not the same," Anita explained in a soothing voice. She lowered her head and opened her eyes to gaze into Kenya's. "This boy will not let you down unless you let him."

"But I let Mark let me down without even knowing it," Kenya whimpered. Anita had released her hand, and she placed it in her lap.

"Ah, no, dear," Anita said, standing up and walking around the large table to take the seat next to Kenya. "Betrayal is in Mark's nature. Even if your eyes had been wide open, he would have found a way to deceive you. This new boy is nothing like Mark. He is a good boy. Let him earn your trust."

"Earn my trust?" Kenya repeated, no longer afraid.

"Yes, dear." Anita's eyes crinkled again. "It is the only way to secure a relationship. He must earn your trust, just as you must earn his. But he can do this only if you let yourself go and allow him to catch you."

Kenya smiled as Anita's cryptic words began to sink in. She would never trust Scott if she was suspicious of every little move he made. The poor guy had done absolutely nothing to hurt her; nothing to make her mistrust him. She had no reason to believe his profession of love at the Y on Saturday hadn't been true. Unless she opened her heart and let herself love Scott, she would never feel free when she was with him.

Love him? Do I love him? Kenya felt her heart warm as she thought of his smile, his kiss, his arms around her, holding her up.

Yes, she thought, feeling a huge weight lift from her heart, her shoulders, her mind. *I really do love him!*

Kenya jumped out of her seat, sending it sliding back across the wooden floor.

"Thank you, Anita!" she exclaimed as the old woman rose slowly to her feet. "What do I owe you?" Kenya fished into her purse, her hands shaking in excitement.

"Don't worry, dear," Anita said, placing a hand on Kenya's arm. "Just let me know how it works out."

"I will! I promise," Kenya said, smiling. She turned and bolted through the door, past the flowers, and out onto the sidewalk.

She couldn't wait to find Scott and tell him. She couldn't wait to tell him that for the first time in her life, she was actually in love. With him.

Nine

"**W**HAT DO YOU think, Scott? Do I look better in this light, or over here in the shade?"

I don't really care where you stand, Scott thought as he watched Emma run from the sunlit field over to the trees and back again.

But to Emma he said, "The sunlight's a little harsh. I think the shade is more flattering to your skin tone."

Emma ran back under the shade of the trees that lined the stream at Huff's Park. It was Monday afternoon, and instead of spending his free time working on his project, Scott was at the park near his house taking head shots of Emma. She had told him she wanted to try to break into modeling, but she didn't have enough money to hire a professional photographer to do her book. Scott had agreed to take the pictures, telling himself it would be good experience. But ever since he'd arrived at the park to meet her he'd been silently vowing never to be so nice again.

Scott crouched down to take some pictures from different angles, pressing one bare knee into the soft, warm grass. Emma kept twirling around and lifting her hair and pouting as though she were doing some kind of *Victoria's Secret* layout.

"Emma, would you quit moving so much?" Scott asked in a more irritated tone than he'd intended.

Emma's face fell and she looked at him in wide-eyed confusion. "But that's what models do!" she said with a whine in her voice. It was all Scott could do to keep from rolling his eyes.

"Runway models, yes," he said in a calmer tone. "But if you want good, flattering head shots, you have to sit still so I can take my time and get the light and shading right."

Instantly, Emma's face brightened, and she grinned at Scott flirtatiously, batting her lashes. "Oh, Scott," she gushed, "you know so much about photography. I am *so* glad I asked you to do this!" She rushed over to him and gave him a quick hug.

"Why don't you go sit down on those flat rocks over there?" he asked when she pulled away. She smiled up at him and then moved to the area he had indicated. Scott knelt down next to his bag to fish around for a new lens.

"How's this, Scotty?" Emma drawled. This time Scott did roll his eyes, because there was no way she could see him. He fastened on a zoom lens and turned to look at Emma. She was leaning back on one arm with her tan legs stretched out in front of her. Her skintight white shorts could have passed as a bikini bottom, and she was leaning back slightly, so her blue cropped T-shirt rode up and exposed her perfectly flat stomach. Scott inhaled sharply. Every guy in school would kill to be in his place at that moment.

"You look beautiful," he said, bringing the camera to his eye. And he meant it. But that didn't change the fact that she was acting like a ditz on wheels. Did she really think he would fall for her just because she was being totally forward? It was strange, the way she could so easily shift from treating him like a friend to pursuing him like a predator. He was beginning to realize that she had asked him here just to flirt with him.

After he had taken a few photos, Scott suggested that she get up and go stand next to a large maple tree. Emma complied and sauntered past him, swinging her hips in an exaggerated fashion.

Scott watched her and smiled wryly once her back was to him. *Doesn't she realize how unattractive her obviousness is?* Scott thought. Immediately his mind wandered to Kenya. Her bubbly, full-of-life, unaffected beauty was so much more appealing than Emma's worship-me attitude. And Kenya was so open with her emotions. Even when she was teary, she was much more beautiful than Emma, because she was so expressive, so real. Emma seemed to have only one expression lately—self-satisfaction.

Emma stood under the maple tree and gazed up at Scott. He fired off a slew of pictures, hoping he would run out of film soon. He had this sudden desire to call Kenya and apologize. And if she wouldn't take his calls, well, then he would just have to go over to her house again. *If I have to kidnap her and lock her in my darkroom, I will get her to sit still for five minutes and listen to me,* Scott vowed. *I will tell her I'm sorry for pushing her too fast and that I'll take any relationship she'll give me, even if it means backing off a little.* Scott knew he'd sound pathetic, but he didn't care. Girls like Kenya didn't come along every day—if he didn't find a way to keep her from slipping through his fingers, he'd regret it for the rest of his life.

That's it, he thought as Emma turned and leaned back against the tree, arching to show her midriff again. *I'll track her down as soon as I'm done here.*

"Oops! My sneaker's untied," Emma said suddenly. She bent down to tie the lace on her white tennis shoe.

Scott kept his camera aimed at where her face had been a second earlier and froze.

Kenya had just walked into the viewfinder. She stopped and looked at him straight in the lens.

Unless she tracks you down first, Scott thought.

Emma popped back up, blocking Kenya from his view.

"Where do you want me now, Scotty?" she asked suggestively. She reached up to twist her hair into a knot at the top of her head, and her shirt rode up to an extremely dangerous height.

I'm toast, Scott thought. *Burnt and crumbly toast.*

★   ★   ★

Kenya's heart beat wildly as images of the past few days fired through her mind in rapid succession.

Anita's confident smile. Aimee scolding her because of her mistrust of Scott. Darrel spinning like a playboy in her bedroom doorway. The girl whose picture was in Scott's wallet, at the pizza parlor, hanging all over Scott like a wet T-shirt. The same girl who stood in front of her now, striking poses as if she were being featured in a Madonna video. The same girl Scott had been smiling at and snapping pictures of for the five minutes that Kenya had been watching them.

Why is my life flashing before my eyes? Kenya thought suddenly. *It's not like I'm dying or something.*

She gave herself a mental shake and brushed past the little supermodel wanna-be decked out in Daisy Dukes and strutted over to Scott.

"Hey, Kenya," he said, pulling the camera strap over his head and leaning forward to give her a tentative peck on the cheek.

Kenya grabbed his T-shirt in the middle of his chest and pulled him to her. In the moment before she kissed him, he looked so surprised that she almost burst out laughing. When they parted, he was flushed with embarrassment. This was much better than what she would have been doing if she had bolted the moment she had seen this girl with Scott—which was exactly what she'd wanted to do for a split second, what she would have done before she'd seen Anita. *But I'm strong, I trust Scott, and I'm* much *better-looking than this twig,* Kenya thought, turning to glance at the girl. She almost giggled in giddiness over her own thoughts. For the first time in almost two weeks, she really felt like herself again.

"Emma," Scott was saying as he placed himself between the two girls, "I'd like you to meet my . . . uh, my . . . friend . . . Kenya."

"Friend," huh? Kenya thought. *Well, we'll just see about that.*

She leaned over and shook Emma's hand warmly, making sure to add a little extra pressure to her grip. She was pleased when she saw Emma wince. This afternoon was just getting better and better.

"It's a pleasure to meet you," Kenya said. "I'm sorry I was so rude at Marra's the other day. Something just went down the wrong pipe."

"Oh, that's okay," Emma said quickly. She walked around Scott and Kenya and bent down to snatch up her purse, which was lying next to Scott's bag. "I'll leave you two alone." With that, Emma took off toward a red Toyota Celica parked on the street.

"That's interesting," Scott said as he watched Emma peel away.

"What's interesting?" Kenya asked, smiling at his handsome profile.

"I've never seen her so nervous," Scott replied matter-of-factly.

"It's that fear thing," Kenya said, wrapping an arm around his waist and tugging on a belt loop on his shorts to get him to face her. "It works on the feeble-minded as well as children."

"Hey, don't call her feeble-minded," Scott

protested, but laughed anyway. "I've known her my entire life!"

"Okay! Okay!" Kenya laced her fingers through his and pulled him toward a nearby bench. "I didn't come here to talk about Emma anyway."

"What *are* you doing here?" Scott asked, dropping down onto the bench. "How'd you find me?"

"I can use a phone book too, you know," Kenya teased.

"Yeah, I know," Scott answered. "But this isn't my house."

"Your sister told me where you were, but only after I told her you wouldn't be pleased to see me," Kenya explained.

"Sounds like Catherine," Scott said, nodding. Then he sat up straight and looked at her with a frightened expression. "Why won't I be pleased to see you? What's wrong?"

"Nothing," Kenya answered, placing a hand on his shoulder to calm him. "I could just tell she'd be more helpful if she knew I might make you miserable."

"Wow. You *are* good with kids." Scott smiled.

"Listen, we have to talk," Kenya said, her tone suddenly serious. She reached down and gripped his hand so he wouldn't think she had bad news. She knew her palms were sweaty. She was nervous about what she was about to say, but she didn't care if he noticed.

Scott looked down and studied their entwined fingers as if it were the most fascinating sight in the world. "Shoot," he said without shifting his gaze. "I'm ready."

"I realized something today," Kenya began. She

took a deep breath and surged ahead, staring at the little stream in front of them. "The thing is, I haven't been giving you a fair chance. And I just realized today how totally moronic I've been, and how badly I've been treating you."

She could feel Scott staring at her.

"What?" she asked, her free hand flying up to pat down her hair. "Do I have something hideous growing on me or something?"

"No! No," he answered quickly. "It's just that I was going to apologize to you."

"You were?" she asked. "For what?"

"For saying I loved you the other day," he said, as if it were totally obvious.

"You mean you want to take it back?" Kenya squealed. A feeling of dread washed over her. She slid away from him slightly.

"No!" Scott cried desperately, squeezing her hand. "I mean, unless you want me to. I mean— uh, I don't know what I mean."

"Wow!" Kenya squeezed Scott's hand back. "I've really confused you, haven't I?" She tucked her chin down and stared at the ground, absently digging a hole in the dirt with the toe of her boot. She wished she could turn back the clock and take back all the times she'd run out on him. But she couldn't. All she could do was try to make things right—here and now.

"There's something you need to know," Kenya said bravely. She released his hand and turned on the bench, pulling her legs up to her chin so she could face him. He did the same and they stared into each other's eyes, his exposed knees gently rubbing against her jeans. His eyes were so soft and brown and full of honesty. How could she not trust those eyes? She suddenly felt the need to tell him everything.

"I caught Mark fooling around with another girl," she told him bluntly. Scott's brow creased in sympathy, and he reached out and gently rubbed the back of her hand with his finger, as if by reflex. "And I guess I've been having trouble trusting you because of it. But I want you to know that that's all over now. I've learned my lesson. You're not Mark. You're nothing like Mark."

"You're right about that, Kenya," Scott said seriously. "I would never treat you that way." He gently grasped her wrists.

Kenya awkwardly planted her feet on the ground as he pulled her up. Her nose bumped his cheek and she pulled back only slightly, so she could look directly into his eyes.

"I'm *not* Mark," he said in a husky whisper. "And I *do* love you."

Kenya's heart flew into her throat as his words sent chills racing down her arms, her legs, her back.

"I love you too," she whispered, the words sounding like individual gasps. "And I *do* trust you."

Then he wrapped his arms around her and lifted her off the ground, as if he knew his kiss would make her melt if he didn't hold on. Kenya lost herself in the sweetest, most passionate kiss she had ever experienced. The rest of the world faded away, and all she could feel were his strong arms holding her and his soft lips kissing her as if he would never stop.

It seemed as if days had passed when he lightly replaced her on planet Earth. She still swooned slightly.

Scott reached out and touched her cheek with his fingertips, lightly, almost reverently.

"Kenya Clarke," he said, his eyes piercing through to her soul with their intensity, "you are the only girl for me."

It was just getting dark as Kenya turned the Saturn onto Mine Street. She shivered just thinking about the warmth of Scott's arms around her and the feel of his lips on hers. He was so perfect. Even if he *had* been grinning at Emma like a puppy dog when she found him . . .

No! Kenya told herself. *No negative thoughts.* Scott had told her that he wasn't interested in Emma as more than a friend and that was that. She couldn't expect him to frown and be grumpy when he was hanging around with a buddy. And that was all Emma was to him—a buddy, a pal.

"'Kenya Clarke, you are the only girl for me,'" Kenya whispered, repeating the words that had made her heart practically explode. She pulled into her driveway and hopped out of the car, feeling as light as air as she skipped up the cobblestone walk toward the front door.

I'm skipping! Kenya thought giddily. *I have totally lost my mind. But in a good way.*

Kenya heard a soft chuckle—Darrel and Courtney were standing on the front step, partially shadowed by the setting sun. She stopped abruptly and covered her mouth with her hand to keep herself from giggling and drawing their attention. She turned, the soles of her boots making a slight crunching sound on some loose gravel, and started to tiptoe back to the driveway, figuring she'd cut around to the back door.

"You know, Courtney," Darrel said softly, "you are the only girl for me."

Kenya's heart constricted. She hadn't just heard that. She hadn't just heard her lying, cheating, slimy toad of a brother use the exact same line on Courtney as Scott had just used on her. What did these guys have, a course on how to scam girls or something?

For the second time that day, images of the past two weeks flooded Kenya's mind. But this time she saw them in a whole new light. Tears clouded her vision as she made her way around the garage in the rapidly darkening night.

Mark and the pixie girl. Emma posing provocatively under the tree while Scott looked on. Darrel's cocky grin as he prepared for a date with Jenn. Emma, once again, hanging all over Scott. But this time there was a new element. This time she could have sworn she remembered Scott doing more than simply smiling—he'd been gazing at Emma admiringly, appreciatively.

I've known her my whole life. Scott's words in defense of Emma reverberated through Kenya's mind as she burst through the back door and slammed it shut behind her with a resounding bang.

What am I going to do? she thought wildly, blowing by her mother and racing upstairs to her room. She was vaguely aware of her mom calling after her.

"Honey? Are you all right?"

No, I'm not, Kenya answered mentally, throwing herself onto her bed as her mind continued to race. Ten minutes earlier she had been totally trusting, and now she didn't know what to think. Why couldn't things just be simple? Why did she have to keep finding similarities between the guy she loved and Darrel and Mark—the biggest slimeballs in Chicago?

No. I don't think I'm ever going to be all right again.

Ten

"YOU'VE HAD ONE too many volleyballs spiked at your head, my friend," Aimee said as she slid into a chair in the cafeteria.

"Come on!" Kenya protested, taking the seat across from her friend. "It's the perfect plan."

"Yeah. If you want him never to speak to you again," Aimee countered. She struggled to cut through her bagel with a flimsy plastic knife.

Kenya sighed in frustration and tore her milk carton open. For the past two days she had studiously cut her phone conversations with Scott short without letting on that anything was wrong. She had also spent a lot of time practicing spikes against the garage wall, which always helped her think. Finally she had come to the conclusion that she had to find out once and for all if she could trust Scott. Darrel's behavior had opened her eyes. He'd told Courtney she was the only girl for him, and had then probably gone inside to call Jenn and tell her the same thing. It was totally possible that Scott had something going on with Emma, or someone else for that matter. Kenya was determined to find out before she had a repeat of the scene with Mark.

After hours of turning the possibilities over in her mind, Kenya had finally come up with a solution to her trust problem—a plan that would set her fears to rest once and for all. The only snag was, the plan involved Aimee, and she was being as stubborn as a mule.

"If you were really my best friend, you'd do this for me," Kenya said, moodily dunking a chocolate chip cookie in her milk.

"Don't even *think* about trying to pull that on me again! The last time I fell for that, I wound up stuck in detention for a week," Aimee continued. "Besides, if I do it, you'll never be able to introduce me to him as your best friend. And what kind of relationship would you have then?"

Kenya bit her lip. She hadn't thought of that. And it would just create a million problems if she had to try to keep Scott and Aimee apart for the rest of her life.

"Well," she said finally, "I'm sick and tired of running around crying like a drama queen. And this is the only thing I can think of that will make me feel one hundred percent secure. I'll just have to find somebody else to do it."

"Ha! Good luck. You'd have to be insane to agree to do that!"

"Agree to what?"

Kenya and Aimee looked up to find Monica

131

Thomas standing at the end of the table, holding a tray of salad and mineral water. In her black minidress and stacked heels, her lustrous hair pulled back, Monica looked as much like a cover girl as ever. But to Kenya she looked like much more—she looked like the answer to her prayers. Kenya shot a glance at Aimee, who returned a sly smile.

"Monica!" they said in unison.

"Sit down." Aimee pulled her backpack off the yellow plastic chair to make room for their victim.

"What's going on?" Monica asked suspiciously, placing her tray on the table, then twisting the cap off her water bottle.

"I have a little proposition for you," Kenya said, leaning forward and lowering her voice conspiratorially.

Kenya launched into an abbreviated story of her thus far rocky relationship with Scott. Monica listened intently to the entire narrative, including the details of the plan that followed. She was so rapt with attention that she had her plastic bottle poised halfway to her mouth the entire time.

"You know," Monica said when Kenya had finished, "that just might work."

Kenya shot a triumphant look at Aimee, who took a bite out of her apple and rolled her eyes in return.

"So you'll do it?" Kenya exclaimed.

"What makes you think he'll even find me attractive?" Monica asked.

Kenya pointed to a table of sophomore guys who were drooling in Monica's direction. When Monica turned to look at them, they all blushed and became instantly mesmerized by their lunches.

"I rest my case," Kenya said.

"All right. But what's in it for me?" Monica asked, stabbing a tomato with her fork.

"What do you mean?" It had never occurred to Kenya that Monica might want something in return.

"Oh, come on, Ken," Monica said, chewing thoughtfully. "I know a prime opportunity when I see one. How about private practice time with you for two hours a week?"

Aimee snorted with laughter.

Kenya's mouth dropped open. "Are you serious?"

"*And* you fake injury at least once before the end of the season and tell Harrington to rotate me into the game in your place," Monica finished, punctuating the offer by stabbing the air with her fork.

"Oh, this is rich," Aimee said, overcome with laughter.

Kenya shot a withering look at Aimee, then turned to look Monica directly in the eyes. "Deal," she said.

"*Really?*" Monica squealed, nearly jumping out of her seat in delight.

"Really?" Aimee repeated.

"Really," Kenya confirmed. "Scott means enough to me that I could make that tiny sacrifice."

He'd just better pass my little test, Kenya added silently, *or I'll have to wipe that beautiful grin right off his face—permanently.*

Scott was sitting in the gallery on Friday afternoon after school taking notes for his photography

133

project. His hand shot across the paper as he scrawled his thoughts rapidly in his large, jagged script. He couldn't believe how easily the ideas were coming to him. At this rate he'd have his project finished by the end of the weekend. *And then I'll have even more time to spend with Kenya,* he thought, smiling as he flipped to a new page in his notebook.

Unfortunately, he'd talked to Kenya only a couple of times since Monday afternoon. She'd been pretty busy with practice and exams, and he'd been distracted by work. But he was looking forward to spending some time with her Saturday evening. He was so psyched they had gotten everything straightened out. Now that he knew how Kenya felt about him, and that she actually trusted him, he could really concentrate on other things, such as getting his project finished. Everything was falling into place.

Scott looked up to study the next picture in the photographic essay he was working on. Somehow a girl had walked into the room without him noticing and planted herself right in his line of vision. *Wow, I must've been more wrapped up in my work than I thought.* Scott stood up and walked closer to the display so he could see the photograph.

As he positioned himself a few feet away from the girl, she glanced at him out of the corner of her eye, then quickly looked away. Scott tried to keep from smiling and continued to take notes.

She's checking me out, he thought.

He walked behind her to view the picture from another angle, taking a closer look at the girl as he went. She wasn't bad—she definitely had a great body. But she couldn't hold a candle to Kenya's unique beauty.

"Are you a photography student?" the girl asked suddenly, looking at Scott with wide eyes.

"Yeah. I'm working on a project," Scott answered.

"I'm thinking of taking up photography myself," the girl said, turning to face him. "I find it so . . . fascinating."

Scott realized she was openly flirting with him. She was staring at him with a coy expression and her voice was deep and sultry. *Unless that's her normal voice,* Scott thought. *But she can't be more than fifteen, so that's hardly possible.*

He was flattered and felt his cheeks flush a little. It wasn't every day a random beautiful girl flirted with him.

"That's great," he said finally, realizing he should probably react to her comment.

"So," she said batting her thick eyelashes. "What kind of camera do you think I should get if I'm just starting out?"

"Well, you'd want to get a thirty-five-millimeter," Scott said, eyeing her to try to discern if she really was interested in photography. "You can get a pretty basic one relatively cheap. Then if you decide you really enjoy it, you can go for something more technically advanced."

"What would a more technically advanced one have—like, different lenses or something?" the girl asked. She sauntered over to the bench Scott

135

had vacated and sat down, crossing her incredibly long legs at her ankles.

"Yeah, something like that," Scott answered with a bit of a smirk. He always forgot that most people knew nothing about photography. Since it was practically his life, he was surprised when someone didn't know the basics. He sat down next to her on the bench and stuffed his notebook into his backpack.

"When it comes to lenses," he began, "there're all different kinds of zooms. Then there's telephoto, and then you can get cameras that will produce panoramic photos, and—"

"Whoa!" the girl said. "This sounds really complex."

Scott laughed. "Well, not really. It's pretty easy to catch on if you're into it."

"Maybe we could get together sometime and you could explain it to me," the girl suggested. She was looking up at him through those lashes again. Scott felt sweat pop up on his palms, and he started to fidget nervously with the hem of his flannel shirt.

"I don't think that's a good idea," he said, looking away.

"Why not?" the girl asked. "I bet you're a really good teacher."

Scott swallowed. "I, uh, don't even know your name," he said lamely.

"I'm Monica," she said, laughing lightly. "Will you go out with me now?"

"Well . . . Monica, I have a girlfriend," Scott told her. Maybe that would scare her away. She was pretty and everything, but Kenya was the only girl he wanted to be with.

"Are you going out with her tonight?" Monica asked in that sultry voice. She leaned over him and pulled his notebook out of his bag. Her leg brushed against his, and alarm bells went off in Scott's mind as his temperature shot up a few degrees. *What is with this girl?* Scott thought frantically.

"No. As a matter of fact, I'm not," Scott said, staring at her hands as she opened his notebook. She grabbed the pen that he had stuck inside the metal spiral binding and pulled the cap off with her teeth.

"Then there's no reason why we can't get together tonight. Is there?" He watched as she wrote down her name and number on the corner of a piece of paper and then tore it off, offering it to him with an extremely flirtatious smile. There was no denying this girl was the textbook definition of gorgeous. But somehow Scott was repulsed. He couldn't believe how she was throwing herself at him. It was time to get away from this girl—as quickly as possible.

"Thanks, but no thanks," Scott said confidently, standing up and lifting his notebook out of her hands. "I love my girlfriend, and I'm not going to go around behind her back. It's just not my style. But thanks for the offer."

Scott started to back away, and Monica stood up. She stepped toward him, slipped the scrap of paper into his shirt pocket, and patted it once with her palm.

"Just in case you change your mind," she said slowly.

Then she winked, twirled on her heel, and walked away.

"Yeah. Whatever," Scott muttered under his breath.

Scott shook his head. He was so glad he had Kenya now. If that was the kind of girl there was out there, all men should be afraid . . . very afraid.

What a mental case, he thought as he grabbed his jacket and headed for the exit farthest from the one Monica had taken.

As Scott pushed through the glass doors and walked out onto the sidewalk, he almost laughed out loud. He could just imagine Kenya's face if she had seen that little episode. *She probably would've attacked that girl,* he thought, *but if she had seen me shoot Monica down, we'd really never have to worry about trust again.*

Scott felt a sudden surge of energy and picked up his pace as he headed for the el. He couldn't wait to call Kenya. Maybe he could ditch his movie plans with his friends for the night and he and Kenya could do something together.

As he raced past a coffee shop at the end of the block, Scott saw a flash of red out of the corner of his eyes and slowed down for a second. *That looked like Kenya's jacket,* he thought.

He stopped and peered through the glass pane of the trendy restaurant. It would just be too cool if she was actually there.

That was Kenya all right.

She was sitting in a booth and drinking a toast . . . with the girl from the gallery! A third girl walked over from the counter and joined them as they lifted their colorful mugs and laughed.

Scott's thoughts raced as he tried to wrap his mind around the scene before him. He was barely aware of the pedestrians rushing past, not even flinching when a woman ran over his foot with a stroller and kept going.

They look like they're celebrating, Scott thought. *But why? How do they know each other?*

Kenya threw her head back and laughed as the coffee shop door opened. The sound sent a shudder of realization down his spine.

"They're laughing at me," he whispered. "*She's* laughing at me."

It was all a setup.

Kenya probably *had* seen the whole thing—but she had probably also written the script. Scott clenched his fists in frustration. *What was it, some kind of test?* he thought, biting the inside of his cheek. *That must've been it. She must have been testing me to see if I'd follow Monica out of the gallery with my eyes popping out of my head and my tongue hanging down to the ground. That's how little she thinks of me.*

All of that stuff on Monday about how she totally trusts me was a lie, he realized, his heart sinking.

"Well, you won," Scott said levelly as Kenya took a sip of her victory coffee. "Now you know you can trust me."

Scott jerked the strap of his backpack to tighten it and squared his shoulders. Then he turned his back on the coffee shop and Kenya and walked away. "But now I'll never trust *you* again."

Eleven

CONSIDERING HE WAS usually such a level-headed person, Scott was having a really hard time dealing with the fact that he was still fuming when he walked into his darkroom later that afternoon.

"I have never *been* so angry!" he yelled, swinging his backpack into the corner with a thud. He flung himself into his rolling chair and went careening against the wall.

"Okay, deep breaths," he said as he placed his elbows on his knees and rested his head in his hands. He inhaled slowly and counted to ten, then exhaled heavily.

The entire way home he'd tried to think of some other explanation for the gathering he had witnessed at the coffee shop. Maybe Kenya knew Monica from school. Maybe they had just randomly bumped into each other. But that didn't explain what Kenya was doing on the same block as the gallery. She had told him that she was going out with her family that afternoon and that she would call him when she got back. So unless Kenya and Monica were sisters and that other girl was an adopted cousin or something, she had definitely lied to him.

"And *she* doesn't trust *me!*" he exclaimed indignantly, standing up and crossing the room to grab some undeveloped strips of film that were hanging near the wall. If he didn't keep moving, he might explode. Maybe he would calm down if he got to work.

Scott began to transfer the images from the negatives onto photographic paper with his enlarger. He shook his head as he realized he had picked the film containing Emma's head shots.

Within minutes he was ready to place the first few pictures into the developer solution. As he walked the photo paper over to the tubs of liquid, Scott realized he was starting to breathe more easily. He slipped the paper into the developer and watched the image float to life, as if by magic. Emma's likeness sharpened, and Scott smiled slightly. The shot wasn't bad. She was staring up at him from the tub with her classic flirtatious smirk.

Scott had hung the photos of Kenya and the kids from the Y up to dry a couple of days ago. Now his eyes rested on a particular favorite. Kenya was kneeling on the gym floor between Ian and Stephanie, but she was looking right at him. Her eyes were bright and shining, and her beauty was breathtaking. Scott smiled in spite of himself.

But just as quickly he was hit with a wave of

nausea. *How could you humiliate me like that?* he thought, staring daggers at her photo.

Emma's eyes were so easy to read—they were all confidence and flirtation. He'd always thought Kenya's eyes were open and innocent, but now he saw them in a new light—there was something more there. Scott squinted, trying to see the cunning and manipulation he had discovered in her that afternoon. But with a start, he realized the hidden quality was something else altogether—it was vulnerability.

Even after all those times she had run off crying, even after she had opened his heart to him at the park, he had never seen her look as vulnerable as she did in this photograph.

Suddenly he felt protective. "What did this Mark guy do to you?" he asked her image. Then he plopped himself back into his chair. "No, no, no!" he growled at himself. "She knows you're not him. She said she loved you and then she stabbed you in the back. You are not allowed to stop being mad at her!"

Yet Kenya was so perfect. So beautiful and interesting and full of life.

"But I'm *so* furious!" he said through clenched teeth, spinning around in his chair to face the opposite wall.

"What am I going to do?" he whimpered.

"I am going to call him as soon as I get home," Kenya said excitedly as she drove through the suburban Chicago neighborhood where Aimee and Monica lived. "Maybe we can still go out tonight."

"Look at you, all giddy and smiley," Aimee grumbled from the backseat of the Saturn, where she was mushed into a ball. "I wish you would just drive faster before I develop a permanent slouch."

Kenya and Monica laughed. "Sorry, girlfriend. That's what you get for being the short one," Kenya told her.

"I'm five-six," Aimee shot back. "It's not my fault you two are tall freaks of nature."

Kenya grinned as she pulled into Aimee's driveway. She jumped out to pop the seat forward, and Monica and Aimee climbed out.

"I can walk from here," Monica said, pulling her purse out of the car. "It's only a couple of blocks." Monica gave Kenya a quick hug.

"Thank you *so* much," Kenya said, hugging her back. "Not only did you execute your role perfectly, but it was an honor to see you in action. No wonder guys follow you around like puppy dogs." Kenya and Aimee had watched Monica's performance from a hiding spot behind a divider in the gallery. Her flirting technique had been utterly impressive.

"Well, the important one was able to resist, and that's all that matters," Monica said with a giggle. "So I'll see you on Sunday for those two hours of practice?"

Kenya rolled her eyes but smiled. "I'll be there with knee pads on."

"See you then! Bye, Aimee!"

"Bye," Aimee mumbled as Monica waltzed off across the lawn.

"What's your problem?" Kenya asked. She

leaned back against the car and crossed her arms over her chest. "Everything went like clockwork."

"I just can't kick this feeling that somehow this is all going to blow up in your face," Aimee said, leaning next to her.

"How?" Kenya demanded. "He passed with flying colors."

"I don't know." Aimee shrugged. "I don't think you should play games with love. It's too dangerous."

"Well, thank you, Ricki Lake," Kenya said good-naturedly. "Now, please excuse me so I can go home and call my true-blue man."

Aimee turned to give Kenya a quick hug. "I really am happy for you," she said.

"Thanks, Aim." Kenya slid behind the wheel and closed the door. "I'll call you tomorrow."

Kenya glanced in the rearview mirror as she drove away and saw Aimee watching her with a worried expression.

"She's like a nervous grandmother," Kenya said to herself with a laugh, turning the stereo to her favorite station. She sang along with the radio and tapped out the beat on her steering wheel as she drove along. Nothing was going to get her down now. She felt as free as a bird.

Kenya sighed contentedly as she pulled into her driveway and flipped down the vanity mirror. She wanted to see what pure joy looked like. She grinned at her reflection. "He passed!" she told herself giddily.

"He passed, he passed, he passed," she chanted, sauntering up the walk and through the front door.

"Kenya, if that's you, dinner's ready," she heard her dad call from the kitchen.

"I'll be right down!" she yelled, taking the steps two at a time. She bounded into her room and grabbed the phone, giggling as she dialed the number. *I feel like I just won the lottery,* she thought as she waited for someone to pick up.

"Hello?"

"Hi, Scott!" Kenya's heart caught when she heard his voice.

"Oh, hi," he said curtly.

She stopped smiling as soon as she noticed the shift in his tone. "What's wrong?" she asked.

"Nothing."

That always meant something.

"Is there anything you want to talk about?" She twisted the red telephone cord around her index finger. "Is everything okay with your project?" Kenya hoped he had gotten enough done before Monica had interrupted him. Maybe she had disturbed his flow.

"The project is fine. I have to go." He sounded really upset. His voice was shaking.

"Okay, well, then I guess I'll see you tomorrow, right?" Kenya's pulse was racing with fear, but she tried to force some brightness into her voice.

"Yeah, okay." *Click.*

Kenya was frozen in place as she listened to the dial tone hum loudly in her ear. She frantically thought back through the past few days, replaying each phone conversation, trying to figure out if she'd said anything to make him mad. *Maybe he noticed I was purposely rushing through those calls,* she thought, staring at her bedspread. The phone started to beep obnoxiously, and she slammed the receiver down. That had to be it. She took a deep breath to slow her heartbeat and picked up the phone again to dial Aimee's number.

"I think a celebratory mall trip is in order," Kenya declared with forced cheer when she heard Aimee's voice.

"What? Lover boy didn't want to get together tonight?" Aimee teased.

Kenya's stomach turned. She hadn't even gotten far enough to ask. "He already had plans," Kenya said, standing up and beginning to pace. "But we're definitely getting together tomorrow."

"Are you okay?" Aimee asked, concern evident in her voice.

"I'm fine. I just can't talk long 'cause I have to go down to dinner." Kenya stopped walking around and looked at herself in the full-length mirror on her bedroom door. Maybe she should get a fresh new outfit so that she could stun Scott into forgetting about her rude behavior. "So are you in or not?"

"You know me," Aimee answered. "Shop or die."

"Cool," Kenya responded. "I'll pick you up at seven-thirty." She slammed the phone down without waiting for an answer. There was no way she was going to let Aimee get in another probing query.

"When I see him tomorrow, I'll just apologize for being so distracted this week, and it'll all be fine," she said to her reflection.

But for some reason she didn't quite believe it. There had been a quality in his voice that worried her—a coldness she would have thought impossible for him to create. Kenya tried to summon up the confidence she wanted to feel. "Everything will be fine."

She swung open her bedroom door and started down the stairs for dinner. The smell of her dad's famous spaghetti sauce and garlic bread wafted through the house, and Kenya inhaled deeply.

"My favorite meal," she said as she shrugged out of her red barn jacket and threw it over the banister. "See? Everything is just great." She walked into the dining room, looked at the huge bowl of sauce, and grimaced.

So why do I feel sick to my stomach?

Twelve

"WHO DIED?"

"Huh?" Scott looked up to find Jeff flipping a chair around and straddling the back.

"We just saw, like, the funniest movie ever made, and you hardly cracked a smile the whole time. What's the deal?" Jeff rested his arms on the food court table and raised his eyebrows at Scott.

"I guess I just wasn't in the mood," Scott answered, leaning forward to grab a fry from Jeff's tray.

"You would have preferred an action flick?" Jeff asked. He ripped open three packs of ketchup simultaneously and squirted the contents out on the paper tray mat.

Scott shrugged and let out a sigh. He hadn't laughed at any of the jokes in the film because he hadn't heard a single one. He had spent the entire two hours pondering the current Kenya problem. The more he thought about it, the more he realized that he should just never call her again. Not only was he totally thrown, he was hurt and humiliated as well.

Scott shifted in his seat as a few other friends sat down at the next table. He shot them a little half smile, then focused on a windowpane in the high ceiling above Jeff's head.

What his heart told him was completely different and totally irrational. It was telling him to give her another chance.

"Hey, you guys!" Scott turned at the female voice—it was Emma, lowering herself gracefully into the chair next to him at the end of the table.

"What's up, Em?" Jeff asked, nudging the tray in her direction.

"I'm freezing," Emma answered, grabbing a fry. "Can I borrow your jacket, Jeffrey?"

Emma was wearing a tiny white minidress and strappy sandals, even though she had to have known that there would be air-conditioning-induced sub-zero temperatures in the mall that night. She had probably planned ahead so that she'd get the chance to borrow Jeff's coveted suede jacket. If every guy in Scott's school was after Emma, then every girl was probably after Jeff.

Jeff shrugged out of his brown suede jacket and handed it to Emma with a smile, carefully making sure that his precious leather stayed clear of the ketchup.

"So, Scott," Emma said with a serious expression, "there's something I have to tell you."

"What's that?" Scott asked. He leaned back on two legs of his chair and put his hands behind his head.

"You've missed your chance. I've moved on," Emma told him with a slight nod.

She looked so serious and absolutely sorry for him that Scott almost burst out laughing. "How will I ever be strong enough to go on?" he asked mournfully. Then he made the mistake of looking at Jeff out of the corner of his eye. When he saw the expression of pure amusement on his best friend's face, he was consumed by uncontrollable laughter. Scott laid his forehead on the table and shook with mirth, pretending to cry, as Jeff clapped him firmly on the back.

"It'll be okay, Scotty, you'll see," Jeff said in an overly dramatic tone. "We'll get through this together."

"Ha, ha, you guys. Very funny," Emma said testily. She chucked a french fry at Jeff, hitting him in the center of his forehead and sending him into further convulsions.

Scott wiped his eyes. It was a relief to laugh—his anger had almost receded. After sitting in the darkened movie theater all that time, he now just felt tired and confused. He had to figure out what to do next.

Scott looked up at his present company and was suddenly struck with an idea. He was sitting with the two most accomplished daters in his school. Two of the most popular, attractive—if arrogant—people he knew. Why not tap their experience?

"Jeff, Emma, I have a little story to tell you," Scott began, leaning forward slightly. "It's about Kenya." His two other friends leaned in a bit as well, catching the note of seriousness in his tone. Quickly Scott related the details of that afternoon's drama. As he got to the end he began to feel a little embarrassed by what had happened to him. But if he didn't give them all the details, they wouldn't be able to help him decide on his next move.

"I *knew* that girl was no good," Emma said the moment he finished. Jeff pushed back in his chair with his long legs sprawled out under the table and sighed.

"Whaddaya mean, you *knew* she was no good?" Scott asked, shooting Emma a dirty look. "You talked to her for what, five seconds?"

"Calm yourself," Emma said, folding her arms and cuddling into Jeff's jacket. "You've really got it bad, don't you?"

"What makes you say that?" Scott asked warily.

"Because the girl totally played you and you're still defending her," Jeff answered matter-of-factly.

"True love," Emma agreed with a sharp nod, causing her long brown ponytail to bounce.

Scott rested his head in his hands and studied the little knife marks in the white Formica table. He knew his friends were right. He was in love with Kenya. But how could he ever trust her now? How could he ever look at her without remembering that heart-wrenching feeling he had experienced when he'd seen her in the coffee shop that afternoon? He needed to do something. He needed to take action. He needed . . .

"Revenge."

Scott looked up, startled. Jeff had a mischievous glint in his eyes—a glint that over the years had meant nothing but trouble for Scott. After catching

151

a glimpse of that glint before, Scott had ended up with a $150 traffic ticket for doing double the speed limit in his mom's car, had gotten stuck in the top of a maple tree on Halloween and had to wait for the fire department to get him down, and had been caught dyeing his mother's brand-new white sheets a deep red so that he and Jeff could play Superman.

Scott knew better than to listen to Jeff when he had that look. But then he remembered Kenya's heart-stopping smile, her huge brown eyes, her total vivaciousness. He would risk anything to be with her free of spite and suspicion.

Scott leaned into the table again, and Emma and Jeff followed suit.

"What did you have in mind?" Scott asked.

"What do you think of this hat?" Kenya asked as she twirled in front of a three-way full-length mirror.

Aimee looked up from a rack of sunglasses and burst out laughing. "You look like Huck Finn," Aimee declared.

Kenya looked at her reflection dejectedly. The floppy straw hat had seemed sophisticated a minute ago, but now she realized Aimee was right. All she needed was a corncob pipe. Wait—that was Frosty the Snowman, wasn't it?

"Oh, forget it," Kenya said, tossing the hat toward the display like a Frisbee. It sailed over the hat tree and landed softly in a bin of discounted socks. "I might as well give in and go to the Gap. It's not like I ever buy anything anywhere else. I'm so unoriginal."

"That's absolutely not true," Aimee said. She brought a pair of dark cat-eyed sunglasses to the counter. "Sometimes you buy stuff from Banana Republic."

"Oh, big stretch," Kenya said sarcastically. She watched as Aimee counted out the cash for the glasses and added them to her shopping bag full of purchases.

Kenya sighed. They'd been shopping for two hours and Aimee had hit pay dirt, finding something perfect on sale in practically every department at Macy's. So far, Kenya had bought one pair of panty hose for Darrel's graduation party and one Kit Kat, half of which Aimee had devoured. Even though Kenya was the one who had suggested the shopping spree, it turned out that she just wasn't in the mood.

"You 'bout ready to bail?" Aimee asked, checking her watch.

"Yeah. I think I'm all shopped out," Kenya replied.

They walked together through the entrance and out into the mall. Kenya watched as a couple strode by with their arms around each other, laughing quietly with their faces almost touching. Her heart lurched. She couldn't shake the feeling that something had gone wrong with Scott. Something really terrible.

"What's your deal tonight, Ken?" Aimee asked as they stepped onto the escalator.

"Oh, nothing," Kenya said casually. "I just wish I could've seen Scott tonight."

"I'm sorry my company isn't stellar enough for you," Aimee joked. "Now that you've pulled off the scam of the century, you're thinking you're too good for me, aren't you?" They got off the escalator and started toward the food court, where they could cut through to get to the parking deck.

"I hope you'll be understanding about this, Aimee," Kenya replied with a small laugh. "I never meant to hurt you."

"That's okay. I can take it like a man." Aimee pulled on the hem of her jacket and straightened up, pretending to put on a brave front. They both started giggling hysterically.

"Hey!" Aimee said suddenly. "Isn't that Scott over there by Häagen-Dazs?"

Aimee was right. There he was, sitting at a table, talking to someone. The other person was shielded from view by a large potted plant. He laughed, and Kenya's pulse quickened.

"Good eye, Aim—considering today was the first time you ever saw him."

"Well, you picked a good hiding place at the gallery. I had a great view. And besides, I'm a very good spy," Aimee said in a mock-haughty tone. "We should go over and say hi. You could introduce me."

Kenya swallowed with difficulty. *But he's mad at me,* she thought. *I don't know why, but he's mad at me.*

"Kenya?" Aimee prompted.

"Yeah," Kenya said nervously, her knees shaking ever so slightly. "Let's go say hi."

The two girls started moving toward Scott, slowly arcing around a section of tables. Then, unexpectedly, he stood—and so did the person he was with.

Kenya stopped walking. Aimee smacked right into her.

"What gives?" Aimee asked, irritated.

Kenya held her breath as she watched—watched Emma lean into Scott, laughing. Watched him look down at her. Watched him put his arm around her shoulders. Watched her lead him over to a big group of kids standing on line for ice cream. All she saw was his arm. His hand. His fingers curled around Emma's shoulder.

Tears sprang up, and Kenya grabbed blindly for Aimee's wrist. If she didn't have something to support her, she knew, she would collapse.

"Kenya, calm down," Aimee said worriedly, grasping Kenya's arm. "It's probably nothing. Plenty of guys put their arms around their friends when they're hanging out in a crowd. It's *nothing.*"

Kenya gasped for air. This wasn't happening to her. Not again. There was no way this was happening to her *twice.*

"Couldn't handle more than two," she whispered hoarsely.

"Huh?"

"Monica would've been three," Kenya said, still staring at his back. Their backs. Arms still looped around each other. "Anyone could probably handle two girls. Three would be tough."

"Oh, *come on,* Kenya. You can't be serious. One look at his face and you can tell he's a one-girl kind of guy. He *couldn't* lie with that face." Aimee's voice was getting progressively louder. She was obviously frustrated. "I don't understand why *I* can see that and you, who supposedly love him, can't."

"Let's just go," Kenya said in a monotone without making a move. Her insides were twisting into knots, and she couldn't take deep breaths. *This must be what a heart attack feels like,* Kenya thought.

"No way. We're going over there." Aimee started to pull on the end of Kenya's sleeve.

"No!" Kenya stage-whispered. A feeling of total desperation and sudden claustrophobia seized her. Was the glass dome above their heads coming closer? It sure felt like it. She pulled Aimee back with such force that her friend let out a little yelp. Kenya felt a twinge of guilt, but there was no way she was going to let Aimee drag her over there. She already had Mark's guilty expression burned into her memory forever. She didn't need Scott's as well.

Another realization now exploded in her brain like fireworks, shedding bright light on everything. *He's not mad at me,* she thought suddenly. *He's just too busy to even speak to me for more than five seconds. He couldn't wait to get off the phone with me so he could make plans with* her.

"We're outta here," Kenya said, practically sprinting toward the door.

"But—"

"I don't want to hear it," Kenya called without looking back. She slammed hard into the corner of a table with her thigh but felt no pain. At that moment, even a gunshot couldn't overpower the searing agony that was cutting through her heart.

Thirteen

"Is NOT!"

"Is too!"

"All right. That's it!" Kenya looked at her watch and was psyched beyond belief to find there were only five minutes left in the class. "Everyone put the volleyballs back in the bin and go sit by the wall until your parents get here."

"But Ms. *Cla*-arke, I wanna keep *play*ing," Stephanie whined, tugging at Kenya's shorts.

"Please, Stephanie," Kenya said, looking down at the tiny upturned face. "I have a headache."

"Oh." Stephanie's eyes filled with understanding. "My mommy gets those all the time." The little girl ran over to the wall and plopped down next to her pink Barbie backpack.

"I'll bet she does," Kenya muttered. She heard a laugh and turned to see the guy who had been shooting hoops in the next court all morning shaking his head and grinning as he prepared for another shot. Kenya didn't know what he was doing there—she was supposed to have the whole gym from eleven to twelve. But she hadn't really been up for a confrontation when she arrived and he wasn't bothering anybody, so she had let it slide.

Parents started to arrive, and Kenya walked over to the door to say goodbye as the stream of children hurried past. When the last one was gone she felt her shoulders slump again. Kenya was finding it painful to be alone. Aimee was supposed to pick her up, but she wouldn't be there for another fifteen minutes, because she was coming from an appointment at the hair salon. Kenya had to find something to do.

"You wanna shoot around for a little while?" a male voice suddenly asked.

There was something. Kenya turned around. The basketball guy was striding across the gym toward her. She looked over her shoulder to make sure he wasn't talking to someone else, then turned back to check him out as discreetly as possible. The boy was definitely an athlete, but a tiny bit too short to be a basketball player. He was wearing blue cotton shorts and a white T-shirt, and he had very muscular legs. As he approached she noticed his eyes—they were a deep shade of green, especially stunning considering how dark his skin was. She briefly wondered if they were contacts. Real or not, they were beautiful.

"Well?" he asked.

"Huh?"

He laughed, and his whole face lit up when he

smiled. Instantly Kenya missed Scott with an un-bearable intensity.

"You wanna play or not?" He looked her up and down with amusement. "You look like you could hold your own."

Oh, he had no idea what he was in for. She reached forward and slapped the ball out of his hands, running to the net and executing a perfect layup before he even had a chance to blink.

"One to nothing," she said, shooting the ball at him. "Take it out."

The guy sauntered over to her and thrust out his hand. "I'm Jeff," he said.

Kenya shook his hand. "Kenya."

"Well, Kenya," he said with that killer smile, "prepare to die."

Kenya flashed a genuine grin. This would defi-nitely keep her mind off Scott.

Ten minutes later Kenya grimaced and rolled her eyes shut as the ball swished through the net. "Rematch!"

"Oh, no way. I won fair and square." Jeff drib-bled the ball in front of Kenya and regarded her with a cocky expression.

Normally, being so competitive, Kenya would have been ready to wipe the grin right off his face. But she'd had such a great time during their little one-on-one, she couldn't help smiling back. For the first time since the episode at the mall, she actually felt seminormal. But she still wanted a chance to redeem herself.

"Come on," she said, pushing up the sleeves on her sweatshirt. "What, are you scared or something?"

"The word *fear* is not in my vocabulary," he answered, turning toward the basket and shooting a perfect free throw. "I'll play you again. But on one condition." He reached down to grab the ball.

"And that would be?"

"If I win, you have to go out with me tonight," Jeff said with a flirtatious grin.

Suddenly all the lightness washed out of Kenya and a heavy cloud settled around her shoulders, weighing her down. Her heart felt like stone. The last thing she wanted to think about was guys and dating. She still had a date with Scott that night. And she had no idea how she was going to handle that.

"Kenya?" Jeff prodded when she didn't answer.

"I . . . uh . . ."

What should she say? She looked Jeff up and down quickly, then settled her eyes on the orange hoop above his head. He was undeniably gorgeous. And he seemed like a nice guy. Plus he was athletic and fun and . . . not Scott.

Kenya swallowed and searched her brain for something clever to say to stall him while she tried to figure out her entire life. When she came up blank, she burst into a sudden coughing fit and sprinted for the water fountain in the hallway.

Brilliant, she thought as she listened to her rubber soles slapping against the ceramic tile floor. *Now I look like a complete ditz.*

160

Kenya bent over the water fountain and tried to think. She and Scott were still seeing each other, so technically a date with this Jeff person would be cheating. *But he cheated on* you, Kenya told herself. She straightened up and leaned back against the wall with a huge sigh.

It's nothing, *Kenya.* Aimee's voice played in her mind. *One look at his face and you can tell he's a one-girl kind of guy.*

You have to let him earn your trust, Anita's voice said.

Kenya Clarke, you are the only girl for me.

Had he been telling the truth? After all, Scott was not Darrel. Darrel was a true original, and everyone, especially Darrel, knew it. *Maybe I shouldn't have been so quick to judge him. Maybe I should give him a chance to explain.*

"What am I going to do?" she said in total confusion, bringing her hands to her face.

"Did you say something?"

Kenya parted her fingers. Jeff was standing less than a foot away. She could practically feel the heat emanating from his body. The light from the glass doors shone behind him, shrouding him in a grayish shadow. Suddenly she felt very nervous. Who was this guy anyway?

"No. I mean yes. I mean . . ." Kenya took a deep, shaky breath. "Thanks for the offer, but I think the rematch is out." She tried to look up into his face, but her eyes kept darting in all directions. Was he moving even closer, or was it just her?

He leaned over her and braced one hand on the wall above her head.

"Come on, Kenya. I thought we were having a good time," he said in a low voice. Kenya's pulse picked up. *He's not gonna, like, kiss me or something, is he?* She tilted her head slightly to look under his arm at the doors. Where the heck was Aimee anyway?

"I—I . . . uh . . . I have a boyfriend," Kenya stammered. She inched along the wall away from him, but he followed.

"That doesn't bother me," he said. He moved his hand to her shoulder.

Kenya was just about fed up now. This guy had some nerve. She spun away awkwardly and put some distance between them. "Yeah, well, it bothers me," she said, moving toward the door.

"At least give me your number," he persisted.

"No way," she said through clenched teeth. "Now back off before I test what I learned in my kickboxing class on that inflated head of yours." She had never taken kickboxing in her life, but it sounded good. Plus it worked. Jeff stopped walking and raised his hands in surrender.

Kenya turned and bolted out the door. She prayed Aimee was waiting in the parking lot. She suddenly felt the need for a nice long shower to wash Jeff's cooties off her skin.

"Hey, Kenya!"

She stopped short on the top step and looked up at the sound of her name.

What she saw made her jaw drop. There was

Scott, sitting on the hood of his Jeep. He looked incredible in a white tank top and black athletic shorts—but that wasn't why her jaw dropped. Standing just to his left, looking guilty and absolutely petrified, were Aimee and Monica.

"Hey, man!" Scott said, nodding in her direction.

"Man"? Was he talking to her? And what was Monica doing there?

"Yo, Scott!"

Kenya felt the hairs on the back of her neck stand up when she heard Jeff's voice behind her. She stood perfectly still as she watched Jeff jog over to Scott and slap hands with him. The two guys smiled and started to talk in a low tone.

Kenya's head started to spin. Scott and Jeff knew each other? Her eyes narrowed as they turned to look at her, their expressions full of amusement. She shook her head slightly, looking toward her friends for an explanation. But Aimee and Monica weren't paying any attention to Kenya. They were both gaping at Jeff.

"So, Kenya." Scott was the first to speak. "How does it feel to be played?"

Kenya locked eyes with Scott, who was no longer smiling. Jeff, Aimee, and Monica immediately looked at the ground and started to shift uncomfortably.

Kenya's knees began to shake with nervousness while her face boiled with anger and embarrassment. "You set this whole thing up?" she whispered hoarsely. "You set this up to get me back?"

Scott shrugged. "I had to do something."

"How did you find out?" she asked, her voice

cracking slightly. "How did he find out?" She raised her voice to Aimee and Monica.

Scott moved forward, putting himself between Kenya and her friends as if he were afraid she was going to attack. The two girls didn't say a word.

"They had nothing to do with this," Scott said, stuffing his hands in his pockets. "I figured it out on my own and called Monica this morning. Aimee was just an added bonus. She was in the parking lot when we got here. But you haven't answered my question, Kenya. How does it feel to be played?"

Kenya's heart felt as if it were crumbling into a million pieces. He sounded so hurt and disappointed. She risked a glance into his eyes and quickly looked away when she saw the resentment in them.

"I think it's time for us to go." Kenya heard Jeff's voice, but it sounded far, far away. She watched Aimee, Jeff, and Monica shuffle off. They looked like cartoons. Nothing seemed real but the intense emotion flowing between her and Scott at that moment.

"Explain it to me, Kenya," Scott said harshly. "Explain to me why you had to humiliate me like that. What makes you so sure I'm a liar? What did I ever do to make you so suspicious that you had to make me look like a total fool?"

Kenya winced as he spat out the last words. But she wasn't going to back down. Not this time.

"What about Emma?" she asked, a little more confidence in her tone than she felt.

"Emma?" Scott sounded confused, and his little brow crease was back. She couldn't help noticing how the sun shone on his smooth shoulders, making him look like some kind of beach-boy model. *Don't get distracted,* she told herself.

"Yeah. Emma," she said, shifting her weight from one foot to the other. "I saw you two last night and you looked pretty darn cozy to me. And the other times I've seen you together you always get flustered. What exactly is going on with her?"

"You saw us last night?" Scott asked. "Where? At the mall? Were you spying on me again?"

"No! Aimee and I were just there and we saw you put your arm around her and I just thought . . ." Kenya gave up and stared at the ground, suddenly realizing how stupid she sounded.

"Kenya." Scott reached out and took her hand. Kenya felt a warm tingle rush past her wrist and up into her shoulder blades. "I've told you before, Emma and I are just friends. The reason I got weird when you saw us together was, well, because she liked me for a while and she can be pretty aggressive. I didn't want you to see her do something and have you take it the wrong way. Which, I guess, is exactly what happened."

"So you've never gone out with her—I mean, except to that formal?" Kenya asked, staring at their entwined fingers.

"I swear, I never have," Scott answered.

"Oh," Kenya whispered, not knowing what else to say.

"But there's one thing I don't understand," Scott said in a lower voice. He stepped a little closer, and she could feel his breath on her neck, warming her slightly. "If you wanted to know what was going on, why didn't you just ask me? Why are you always running away?"

Kenya suddenly felt weak. She dropped his hand and plopped down on the step. She realized with a start how lucky she was that Scott was there at all. After the stunt she'd pulled on him the day before, she was the last one who should be feeling self-righteous. What had she been thinking? She had assumed it was the perfect plan. But it had done nothing for her. If it had worked the way she'd imagined it would, she wouldn't have been remotely suspicious when she saw him with Emma. Plots and plans were not the way to go. If this relationship was ever going to work, she was going to have to take risks. Risks that involved walking up to her boyfriend in a crowded mall, not hiding behind a wall at a gallery spying on him.

"I don't know," she answered finally as Scott sat down next to her. "I guess I just thought that running away would be easier than finding out for sure that my suspicions were right." She stared at her sneakers, ashamed of her dishonest and silly behavior. "Do you think you'll ever forgive me for being such an immature jerk?" she asked quietly.

"You have to promise me something, Kenya," he said tentatively. She looked up—his face was inches from hers.

"Anything," she answered, catching her breath in her throat.

"I know I can't ask you to just trust me, because that's something that will come with time," he said, his tone serious. "But I need you to at least give me the benefit of the doubt. I need you to be honest about how you feel. I can't take any more of this guessing and running after you and playing *Mission: Impossible* all over the place."

"I promise I will be up front with you from now on," she said, meaning every word. "And I won't ever run away again. Unless, of course, you breathe on me after eating at Marra's."

Scott grinned. "In that case, I think you've learned your lesson."

"Really?" she squeaked. Relief washed over her, and the tension receded from her body. He was going to give her another chance!

Scott laughed and took Kenya's hand. "The way I figure it," he said, leaning closer so their knees touched, "between Jeff and Monica, we're even."

Kenya smiled as she remembered her threat to kick Jeff in the head. *If they're friends, I guess I'll have to apologize to him now,* she thought.

"Besides," Scott said, standing and pulling Kenya to her feet, "we always did really well on dates. It was only the parting that was kind of messy."

"Then maybe we should just never leave each other," Kenya responded playfully. She stepped close to him and wrapped her arms around his neck.

"My thoughts exactly," he agreed in a whisper.

Kenya moaned softly as Scott's lips pressed against hers, gently at first and then more intensely.

She reached up and tickled his neck at the base of his hair until he finally chuckled and pulled away.

"So tell me," he said, wrapping his warm arms more tightly around her waist and smiling down at her. "Did you think Jeff was cute?"

"Ugh!" Kenya wriggled out of his grasp and pulled him by the wrist toward his car.

"What?" he demanded. "You can tell me. Did you or did you not think he was cute?"

"I refuse to answer that question!" Kenya declared, letting go of his arm and running around to the passenger side.

"Why? Because he's the hottest thing you've ever seen?" he continued as they climbed in and he turned the key in the ignition. "I *know* you wanted him, because everybody wants him. All you have to do is admit it and—"

"Scott!" Kenya reached over, grabbed his chin between two fingers, and turned his face to meet hers.

"Yeah?" he muttered through his squished lips.

"Trust me," Kenya said, staring into his eyes. "Jealousy is not worth it."

Scott smiled as best he could with Kenya mushing his face. Finally she released him and leaned in to kiss him deeply. A delightful rush of sensations fluttered down her back and she forgot to breathe for a moment, losing herself in the kiss.

Oh, no, she thought. *There is no way I'm running away from* this *again.*

Fourteen

"I CAN'T BELIEVE this," Kenya said, placing her hands on her hips and looking around.

"Where are we going?" Scott asked. He slipped his arms around her waist from behind and rested his chin on her shoulder.

"When I *want* to find it, I can't find it," she said.

"You don't even know where we're going, do you?" Scott nuzzled her neck.

"Wait!" she said, spotting PJ's Italian Restaurant out of the corner of her eye. "It's over here!" Kenya took off, and Scott trotted after her. She bolted across a street and skidded to a stop in front of a familiar window.

"Anita's Flowers and Fortunes?" Scott asked with unmasked surprise.

Kenya smoothed down her blue cotton blouse and took his hand. "I have to make good on a promise," she said, sweeping open the door and pulling him into the fragrant shop.

"Hello, dears!" Anita looked up from the plant she was misting and smiled.

"Hi, Anita!" Kenya said. She crossed the room to greet the little old woman. "Do you remember me?"

"Of course I do, dear," Anita said. She placed her squirt bottle on a table and wiped her hands on her sweater. She leaned in slightly, as if to whisper in Kenya's ear, but she was so short, her cheek only grazed Kenya's arm. "This is him?"

Kenya nodded and looked over at Scott, who was standing by the door. With both hands shoved in the back pockets of his jeans, he appeared totally uncomfortable. Anita walked over to him, her long black gauze skirt swishing as she moved.

"Come in, child," Anita said, wrapping her arm through his. Kenya noticed he didn't flinch at her touch and once again wondered if the cold shock she had experienced on more than one occasion was all her imagination. "I've been waiting for you," Anita said, smiling up at him. They walked past Kenya into the back room, and Scott shot her a perplexed look over Anita's head. Kenya giggled and followed the pair, noting how dwarfed Anita was by him.

Anita led Scott to the chair in which Kenya had sat the last time she was there. Kenya took the seat next to him as Anita crossed the room and started to prepare three cups of tea from a steaming pot.

"Who is this weirdo?" Scott cocked his head and whispered when Anita turned her back.

"She's not weird," Kenya whispered back. "She's practically the reason we're together."

Scott looked as if he was about to ask another question when there was a clatter on the table in front of them.

"Tea." Anita's offer was more of a demand.

Kenya reached out and took a cup from the tray. Scott followed suit, shooting her a guilty glance. Kenya hoped Anita hadn't heard his remark.

The little white-haired lady slid into the chair across from Scott and stared him in the eyes. "Give me your hand," she said, reaching out her own.

Scott looked at Kenya in confusion, and she nodded. "It's okay," she said.

Gingerly he put his hand forward, and Anita clasped it with hers. Kenya smiled as she watched Scott's eyebrows shoot up and saw him start to squirm. *The cold shock,* she thought.

After a brief moment Anita spoke. "You've found true love," she said, her eyes squeezed shut.

"How much did you pay her to say that?" Scott joked in Kenya's direction. Anita opened her eyes and fixed him with a reproachful glare. He stopped smiling. Satisfied, Anita closed her eyes again.

"Now that you've found true love," Anita continued, "it will give you the strength to accomplish anything. I see great success in your future." She released his hand and gave him a slight nod.

"That's it?" he asked, pulling his arm back. "That's all you're gonna tell me?"

Kenya noticed that he wasn't as calm and cool as he sounded. As he reached for his teacup his hand was shaking.

"That's it," Anita said, getting up and rounding the table to stand next to his chair. "And one piece of advice," she whispered, just loud enough for Kenya to hear. "Don't mess this relationship up."

"Or I'll regret it for the rest of my life?" Scott asked.

"Or I'll come after you," Anita replied, narrowing her ice blue eyes.

Scott gulped, and Kenya cracked up. Anita winked at her and started for the back of the room. Kenya tried to control her laughter as Scott shifted in his seat.

"And dear?" Anita said, her hand on the knob of a door marked Private.

"Yeah?" Kenya asked, stifling her giggles.

"Don't you mess up either," Anita finished with a smile. "He's a keeper." With that, Anita disappeared from the room, letting the door shut noiselessly behind her.

"Let's get out of this creepy place," Scott whispered, jumping up.

"I don't see what's so creepy about it," Kenya said, following him through the jungle of flowers and out the front door. "She's right about you being a keeper."

"Yeah, well, she was right about something else, too," Scott said, taking her hand. His shoulders visibly relaxed.

"What's that?" Kenya asked.

"The success in my future," he answered.

"Well, duh," Kenya said. "We already know that you got the internship." The photo editor at the *News-Tribune* had called that morning with the good news.

"But that's not all," Scott said with a conspiratorial grin. "Now it's my turn to surprise you."

"I *really* wish you would take your hands off my eyes," Kenya said for the umpteenth time as she carefully put one foot in front of the other.

"It's all good," Scott whispered in her ear. "I won't let you maim anybody."

"Where are we going?" Kenya whined. She knew they were in the gallery, because he hadn't insisted on covering her eyes until they were inside. But she couldn't figure out which room they were in because he'd taken her through so many turns. She heard people whispering all around her and wondered just how idiotic she looked.

"*Please, Scott!*" she said through clenched teeth, jumping up and down a couple of times for emphasis.

"Okay! Okay! We're here. Geez, I'd hate to see you on Christmas morning," he said, removing his hands.

Kenya blinked a few times as she tried to focus. Her eyes rested on a huge banner draped across the wall in front of her. It read Winners of the Young Artists Competition in huge red letters. Her heart started to pound. Had Scott won something? Stepping closer to the wall, she scanned the photos one by one until she found something that made her gasp.

Her own eyes. Her own eyes were staring back at her from a huge black and white photograph.

Kenya looked back at Scott in total disbelief. He

grinned mischievously and walked over to stand next to her.

"I don't believe it," she whispered. Her face filled the entire photograph, her eyes bright and innocent. She reached out and touched the frame lightly with the tips of her fingers, mesmerized. She felt completely flattered and proud at the same time.

"Check it out," Scott said, indicating the little card next to the picture.

Kenya leaned over to read it: "*Trust Me,* by Scott Hutson. First-place winner." She looked up at him. "First place?" she repeated, looking up at him. "Scott, that's so incredible! Why didn't you tell me?"

"I didn't know," Scott explained, leading her over to a bench. "I turned in my final project and portfolio, and the next thing I know, Mrs. Montagne's telling me she entered my photos in this competition—and I won."

"That's so amazing!" Kenya said. She touched his cheek with the palm of her hand. "You did it! You're showing here, just like your dad!"

"I know," Scott said. "I think he'd really be proud of me."

"*I'm* really proud of you," Kenya said. She leaned forward and wrapped her arms around him, hugging him tightly. She buried her face in his shoulder, inhaling his sweet scent and feeling a comfortable, familiar warmth spread all over her body. She felt as if she were flying—it was definitely one of the happiest moments in her life.

"I couldn't have done it without you," he

whispered. He kissed the top of her head and then pulled back to look in her eyes. "I feel like there's nothing I can't do when you're with me."

Kenya let out a sound that was somewhere between a laugh and a sob. "Well, then I guess what I said the other day was right," she said, blinking back ridiculous tears.

"What was that?" Scott asked, placing his forehead against hers and causing their noses to touch.

"We should never leave each other," Kenya whispered.

"You've got a deal," Scott said huskily. He tilted his head ever so slightly and caught her lips with his own. Kenya's heart filled with hope and love, and she felt herself go weak yet again. She clasped his jacket with her hands and let him support her when he wrapped his arm around her back.

A new wave of emotion washed over her and she deepened the kiss, smiling slightly when Scott let out a little moan of surprise.

She was feeling something she'd never felt before—complete and total trust.

Do you ever wonder about falling in love? About members of the opposite sex? Do you need a little friendly advice but have no one to turn to? Well, that's where we come in . . . Jenny and Jake. Send us those questions you're dying to ask, and we'll give you the straight scoop on life and love in the nineties.

DEAR JAKE

Q: *Brian and I have been friends for years. He's very good-looking, but I could never see him as more than a friend. Recently, I became friends with this great girl named Jamie. At least, I thought she was great. Now it's starting to seem like she only became my friend to get close to Brian. She's always asking me to bring him along when we go out, and she won't stop asking me about him. How can I find out if she wants to be my friend for me or if she's using me to get to Brian?*

RK, Cedar Rapids, IA

A: Being used really stinks. It's possible that Jamie has a thing for your buddy Brian and that's why she's suddenly showing interest in spending time with you. Or maybe she likes both of you and getting to be around him is just a side benefit of your fabulous company.

There is a way to try to feel things out: Ask Jamie to go somewhere with you when you know Brian's busy. Does she want to see that movie even if he won't be sitting on the other side of her? If you're still feeling unsure, you can always come right out and ask her what the deal is. Tell her that as much as you love Brian, you'd rather talk about something else with her for a change. If she sticks around, she's for real.

Q: *There's a guy in my school, Kenny, who I want to ask out. I'm just afraid that he'll say no and then everyone at school will laugh at me. I could deal with being rejected, but I can't deal with being the laughingstock of my school. What should I do?*

SJ, Merrill, WI

A: No one likes to feel embarrassed; in fact, most of us would rather break an arm than be laughed at. It's perfectly natural that you'd be concerned about the reactions of your friends at school . . . but gossip comes and goes faster than lunch period. Even if Kenny does say no to you, by tomorrow it will be old news. It's pretty unlikely that people would laugh at you anyway. There's no reason you should be ashamed of asking a guy out.

On the other hand, Kenny might say yes—

and then you'd be psyched to get the guy and be pretty proud of yourself for being brave enough to go after what you want. Remember, nothing risked, nothing gained.

Q: *My boyfriend, Brandon, and I have been very serious with each other for three years. Recently he told me that although he loves me and wants to end up with me, he feels like he needs to go out and date other people just to know what it's like. I was really hurt, because I don't feel the need to date anyone else—I know Brandon is the one. Is this a normal guy thing, or should I take this as his way of breaking up with me?*

RS, Tulsa, OK

A: I think "normal guy thing" might be an oxymoron. I hate to be a traitor to my gender, but we have some strange ways of dealing with relationships. Yes, it's a *common* male attribute to feel the need to go out and explore. We like to reassure ourselves that we've still got the power to attract girls. Brandon might really feel the same way about you as you do about him, but he needs to prove it to himself in a way that you don't.

I don't think he wants to lose you, because he's told you that he still thinks you're the one he'll come back to. However, you have every right to refuse to sit around and wait for him to find out what you already know—that you two are right for each other. Tell him that the idea of him dating anyone else upsets you, but if he needs to do it, then you'll both need to take some time apart and see what happens. If you are really meant to be together, you'll both realize that in time.

DEAR JENNY

Q: *I'm in eighth grade, and I have this really big crush on my friend Josh. I think I might even be in love with him, but my friends tell me I'm too young to be in love. Do you think it's possible to be in love at my age? How old do you have to be to fall in love?*

AW, Bartlett, TN

A: Maybe I'm just a romantic at heart, but I don't think there's an age limit on love. You have to be sixteen to drive a car and eighteen to vote, but love defies all laws. How old do you have to be? Old enough to care deeply for another person, and to put their happiness up there with yours. I think we are born with that ability.

However, I must say that as you get older,

you are better able to handle a mature and serious relationship. Although it varies and there is no set age for everyone, it does take time to be ready for real commitment. So take your time with Josh; you have plenty of years ahead of you. Never doubt your own feelings, though—if you believe what you feel for Josh is sincere, then it is.

Q: *I'm only fifteen, but when I met my boyfriend, Matt, I told him I was sixteen. He's seventeen and I was afraid he'd think I was too young if I told him my real age. Now we've been together for a month and I feel extremely guilty about lying to him. Should I tell him the truth? I know it's bad to lie to someone you love but I'm scared I'll lose him if he knows how old I really am.*

SG, San Jose, CA

A: Lying is always dangerous because one lie ends up leading to more lies . . . what do you tell Matt on your birthday? I think you realize that if you are going to stay with Matt, you'll need to be honest. Trust is a fundamental part of any relationship.

It's understandable that you're scared of his reaction, but if Matt really cares for you, it won't matter if you're a year younger than he thought you were. He loves you for who you are, not for how many years you've been on this planet. However, even if Matt doesn't care about your true age, he will be upset that you lied to him. Reassure him that you have been absolutely truthful about everything else and that you will not lie to him again. Hopefully he will admire your courage in coming clean and forgive you for your white lie.

Q: *Andrew and I went out for about four months and we had a good relationship. The breakup was pretty much mutual; we both realized things didn't feel right anymore. However, once we broke up we stopped talking to each other. I miss his friendship. I want to call him and see if we can be friends like we were before we ever dated, but I don't know what to say. How do you become friends with an ex?*

RB, Durham, NC

A: A lot of friendships come from fizzled relationships, and some of my closest friends are guys I once dated for short periods of time. It makes sense that you would still like to be in touch with Andrew if the only thing missing between you was the special chemistry that leads to a love connection.

It shouldn't be a problem, since things didn't end badly. Call him up and invite him out to a casual place, like the mall. Even better, invite him out with a group, so he's clear that your intentions are innocent. It might be a little awkward at first, but as long as both of you are over any other feelings, your friendship has a chance.

Do you have questions about love? Write to:

Jenny Burgess or Jake Korman
c/o Daniel Weiss Associates
33 West 17th Street
New York, NY 10011